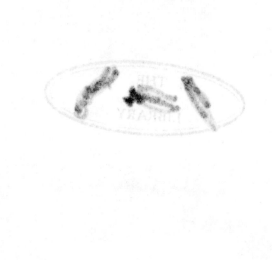

The Fascinator

By Andrew York

The Fascinator

ANDREW YORK

PUBLISHED FOR THE CRIME CLUB BY
DOUBLEDAY & COMPANY, INC.
GARDEN CITY, NEW YORK
1975

All of the characters in this book
are fictitious, and any resemblance
to actual persons, living or dead,
is purely coincidental.

$$\frac{F}{C\ 3}$$

Library of Congress Cataloging in Publication Data

Nicole, Christopher.
The fascinator.

I. Title.
PZ4.N6425Fas3 [PR9320.9.N5]   813
ISBN 0-385-08443-9
Library of Congress Catalog Card Number 74-25131

Contents

"Oh! Death will find me, long before I tire
Of watching you; and swing me suddenly
Into the shade and loneliness and mire
Of the last land!"

Rupert Brooke

PART ONE

The Man Who Killed Women

CHAPTER 1

A military band played, its music brassy as it seeped upwards into the hot desert air. Sweat dribbled down the brown faces and stained the wilting khaki jackets with their red tabs. Every few seconds one of the buglers hit an uncertain note, and the entire morning seemed to quaver.

Behind the band the surf pounded with equal energy on the beach. But here the beach was merely a continuation of the land, brown and arid. The houses were equally brown, equally arid, protruding from the earth like grotesque stalagmites, weathered by age. The town faced the unending ocean, which was hardly more salt than the land out of which the houses had grown with such patient resignation. From a distance, like the ocean, the town looked lifeless.

But like the ocean, it teemed with life, this day mainly accumulated in the central square before the white stucco walls of the Palace of Justice, listening to the band, watching and waiting. Many had come in from the desert, and wore the robes and the burnous of the Bedouin. The nomads were gravely interested in what was about to happen; their women peered over their yashmaks, and even their children were quiet. Death was commonplace, but never spectacular, in the desert.

And the government could count on their support. The band and the equally sweating soldiery who lined the square were there to over-awe the townspeople. For here a certain gayness was evident, an attempt at a Mediterranean cosmopolitanism which failed, not only because the Mediterranean was many hundreds of miles away, but because the people of Xanda had always enjoyed life at second hand.

Until recently. Recently, now, and surely for all the foreseeable future, life was there to be enjoyed. There were only a few motor cars in Xanda, but more were arriving every day, and when the great new dock, bulging seawards from the beach with a gleaming whiteness which put the rest of the town to shame, was completed, the cars would arrive in ever-increasing numbers. So would the washing machines and the dishwashers and the television sets. This had been promised, and this would happen.

Providing everyone was sensible about it. And the people of Xanda, on the whole, were prepared to be sensible. Everything comes to him who waits, and surely they had waited far too long. Only the fools, the anarchists, and the perpetual rebels, the agents of Western imperialism and Eastern ambition, would wish to change things. Thus the soldiers. For there were obvious Europeans in the crowd, and obvious Asiatics as well. Some were well known; there had been British merchants here since the first English warship had needed fresh water from the original oasis, three centuries ago. There had been French merchants here, since the British had shown *their* interest. And in more recent years, there had been American and Russian technicians and drillers, for it was the policy of the Prince not to favour any one side more than the other.

There was also a smattering of tourists. Xanda was still off the beaten track, as yet beyond the reach of the package tours. It was still real. How real these tourists were about to find out.

But no doubt, disguised either as tourists or businessmen or legation officials, there were also people who caused trouble, who wanted Xanda to go in one direction or the other, or perhaps not to go in any direction at all. These were the people the soldiers watched for, because perhaps they would not like to see their comrades die, without protesting.

The moment was at hand. The trucks containing the television cameras had rolled through the crowds, displacing acres of dust into the still midday air, and now the wires had been unrolled and the technicians were ready. There were still no television sets in Xanda, but the rest of the world could not be allowed to miss a public execution.

And now, the Prince was here. The bullet-proof white Cadillac came slowly up the Parade, as the main street was nostalgically called, preceded by its twelve motor bikes and followed by the clattering hoofs of its imperial escort of lancers, burnouses a splash of unexpected crimson midst the browns, green and white pennants fluttering, horses magnificent in their grace and power and effortless energy. The interior of the car was hidden to sight behind the one-way glass, and when the Cadillac stopped at the foot of the steps to the dais, a phalanx of white-coated, crash-helmeted policemen moved forward effectively to shut out the Prince from the gaze of the crowd. Because despite all the precautions, amongst the gazes might be a high-powered rifle, or a bomb; that was what this morning's ceremony was all about.

The Prince mounted the steps, a tall, surprisingly slender figure, shoulders slightly bowed, face hidden because he wore a crimson burnous over his pale grey suit. The other cars had also stopped, and the court ladies and officials, and the ambassadors and their ladies, and the oil bosses and their ladies, were being arranged into rows, carefully standing to attention, Panama hats being removed and held against male breasts, white-gloved female hands clutching white leather handbags against nylon-shrouded bellies, conscious that they were the focus of all eyes, and yet conscious too of the horrific implications of their presence.

The Prince entered the bullet-proof glass box in which his chair was waiting; four guards entered with him, the girl with the fan, the girl with the jug of iced water, and the girl who would taste each cupful. And now the band ceased its martial music, and for five seconds the square and the town, and the people, stood in silence, while the dust left by the cavalcade filtered through the sunlight, and an occasional horse stamped its feet, and a miasma of sweat and apprehension filled the morning.

Leigh said, "You'd think he was declaring the football season open."

The woman did not answer. Like everyone present, she was watching the far side of the square, where a small gate led into the Palace of Justice itself, and where the soldiers were reinforced by two machine-gun nests. Because now, with perfect timing, a procession approached from within; two dozen policemen, heavily armed, and, lost to sight in their midst, three people. From a distance it was difficult to tell their sexes as they each wore a shapeless prison smock, and they moved shapelessly as well, rather shambling than walking. But two of them had long hair, thin, dark, fluttering in the breeze. Or were there already grey streaks amidst the black?

"Can you imagine," the woman said, "what those bastards must have done to them?"

"Whatever they did to them," Leigh said, "it couldn't have worked. Or we wouldn't be standing here."

"Why are we standing here?" the woman asked. "It is ghoulish."

"Sssh," Leigh said, and straightened his shoulders. For the procession had entered the square, and stopped, and the band was striking up again. Now it was the national anthem, an appropriately stirring tune, which cascaded over the dais and round the Prince, sent the chins of the soldiery a little higher, brought sighs from the populace. "Bloody deafening row," Leigh muttered. And he and the woman were at the back of the crowd, apparently late arrivals, tourists who had been out for a morning stroll and been caught up in the blood heat excitement of the morning.

The music died, and the soldiery was moving again. All of the soldiery. Those lining the walls stroked the barrels of their automatic weapons, and frowned with concentration. Now, if ever, there might be some attempt at revenge. Rescue was not considered a possibility by the authorities.

And the soldiers surrounding the three prisoners were also moving, slinging their weapons as they moved their victims to the three posts, set facing the dais and only a few feet in front of the palace wall.

"Those are civilised people." The woman was gazing at the V.I.P.s. "How can they sit there and watch?"

"Because they have been commanded to do just that," Leigh pointed out. "Right this minute there is no diplomat in the world who is going to risk upsetting the Prince of Xanda."

"They should be out there," the woman said. "Do you know something, Clem? I hate the whole goddamned race. I mean species. Not just that pumped-up twit."

"They say, like Peter the Great, he takes a personal interest in the interrogation of state prisoners," Leigh said. "Especially the female ones." But he was also fascinated. His tongue circled his lips, and he frowned as much as any of the watching soldiers as the prisoners were placed against the stakes, the man in the centre, and the two women on either side. Now they stared at the dais and the crowd, and it was easy to see how young they were. And how frightened.

But now the executioners had also appeared, with the black hoods which they dropped over the three heads. The girls' hair continued to flutter, and their bodies to shake, as the ropes were adjusted and the pieces of wood inserted into the knots. Then the executioners waited, looking up at the dais. The doomed people waited also, their smocks trembling in the breeze, their legs, bare from the knees down, strangely slender and helpless.

And the crowd waited too, almost audibly drawing their breaths, in concert with the three anarchists. Leigh glanced at the woman. But she was caught in the strange intimacy of death, which spread outwards from the dusty square to encompass every man, woman, and child in the audience. Except the Prince. He was nodding, and the wood was being turned. The feet moved, and one of the girls kicked, but only for a moment.

"They say it is very quick," Leigh remarked.

The woman was breathing slowly, her nostrils dilating and then closing again.

The drum roll spread out over their heads and filled their bodies, as the legs went still, and the lifeless forms drooped against the stakes.

"I'm going to be sick," the woman said.

Leigh caught her arm, and was hurrying her up the street before she knew it. "You won't," he said.

Behind them, the music was stopping, and the people on the dais were rising, preparing once again to salute the anthem.

"So," Leigh said. "We'll have to start again."

The woman slumped against a wall, looked up, and seemed to understand where she was for the first time. He had taken her down a side street, and here they were even shaded from the sun.

"You're joking," she said. "It's not possible."

"Everything is possible."

"But . . . for God's sake," she shouted. "We'd never improve on Chad, and the girls. How, Clem? You tell me how. How do you draw a bead on a man you can't even see? How do you poison a man whose every drop of food or wine is pretasted? How do you knife a man when everyone, no matter who he or she may be, is searched before being allowed into his presence? How do you blow up a man who travels only by his own particular transport, which is inaccessible to anyone but his own guards?"

"How do you get yourself garrotted?" Leigh asked. "By standing on a street in Xanda shouting about murdering the Prince."

"Oh, for Christ's sake . . . they don't understand English."

"I wouldn't count on that." He grasped her arm again. "Come on, I'll buy you a drink."

For Xanda was returning to normal. The three bodies were being removed from their posts—only a few years ago they would have been left there for three days, in the tropical heat and beneath the cloudless sun, but it was part of the Prince's ambitious programme of reform to make his country civilised—and the crowd was melting away, still buzzing with excitement, to resume sipping their apéritifs at the French-style street cafes, to mutter knowingly about the all-seeing, all-knowing, all-embracing wisdom of their prince.

"Room service," Leigh said. They were staying at the principal hotel in the city, a large square white building, belonging to an American financier although operated by a Xandan manager and staff. But here, too, the accent was on civilisation, and one of the assistant managers was already hurrying forward to assist as the European couple entered the green and gold foyer. "It is very hot," Leigh explained. "And Madame . . . the executions, you understand."

"I know, monsieur. I know," the assistant manager agreed. "They are not to everyone's taste. Me, I will watch the film." He giggled, seized the woman's hand, and kissed it.

"Champagne," Leigh said. "Two bottles, I think."

"Of course, monsieur. Of course. Immediately."

The woman withdrew her hand at the third attempt, and went to the lift, Leigh at her shoulder.

"Let's hope the damned thing works," she muttered.

It didn't always.

Leigh pressed the right buttons, watched her wilting against the wall. Suddenly he was switched right on. Because, although he would never have admitted it to anyone, much less *her,* he had also felt a little sick, out there in the heat and the stench, and the action. Now, in the air-conditioned cool of the hotel, he could concentrate on the action. On Thelma, having the life expertly squeezed from her exquisite neck. What changes had taken place in her body at that decisive moment?

And then had been final. What had happened to her, before? She had been in the hands of the secret police, the Xandan secret police, an Arab secret police, for nearly a month. Charged with attempting to assassinate the Prince. And, as he had said, the Prince would himself have been there, probing with those soft hands, asking with that soft voice. That set his imagination racing about like an electric Yo-Yo.

That made him want the woman.

She led him out of the lift, across the green and gold carpet of the lobby, and up to the bedroom. He reached past her to unlock the door, kissed her neck as he did so. It was covered in a thick film of sweat, reaching to him through the perfume.

"Christ," he said.

Carmel opened the door and went in. "You are a pervert," she said. "How anyone, even you, could think of sex at a moment like this . . ."

Because she, too, had clearly been thinking about Thelma. Or perhaps about Chad. On reflection, Leigh realised, there was so much that a thoughtful interrogator could do to a man more than to a woman.

"Why don't you have a shower," he said. "And then come and lie down."

She glanced at him and went through to the bathroom. Leigh walked to the french windows, threw them open, and was greeted by a blast of oven-like air. He stepped on to the balcony, closing the doors behind him, looked down at the square and the narrow streets and the dispersing people. In the strongest possible contrast to Carmel, he felt positively exhilarated. He had devoted so much time over the past few years, ever since, in fact, the oil strike, to the destruction of the Prince, he did not really know what he was going to do when at last he was successful. He was a professional anarchist, and the Prince was a professional reactionary, with a professional's interest in survival. They were playing a mental game of chess, the pair of them, without ever having met. Without the Prince, in fact, being aware of Leigh's existence—as Leigh.

He could almost feel the cord tightening around his own neck at the very idea.

But if he was going to win the game, it was necessary to move to the head of the pack. Carmel's outburst on the street had contained too much of the truth. And perhaps there was the true reason for his excitement. Always he had remained in the shadows, directing and manipulating. Now he was down to his original group of five, and they would all have to do their bit, himself most of all. Although

. . . it was just possible that he had discovered a joker. Of course, only a fool would rely on a joker alone to take the hand, but a joker could unsettle the opposition, leave them exposed to an overlooked trump.

Behind him, the door opened, and a waiter deposited the full ice bucket and the tray with the two glasses. Leigh stepped back inside, tipped the boy, made sure the door was locked behind him. He opened the first bottle, filled the glasses, and turned on the piped music. He did not know whether the Xandans were sophisticated enough to have bugged all their hotel rooms, but he was by nature a cautious man, and in any event, these walls were not as thick as they should have been.

He opened the bathroom door. Carmel had finished her shower, and towelled, slowly and thoughtfully, staring at herself in the full length mirror. She was a tall young woman, a natural blonde who therefore found intense sunlight more disturbing than most. At the moment she seemed concerned about a sudden rash of freckles which had appeared on the tops of her breasts. Small breasts, which were curiously attractive on top of the somewhat rangy legs and the wide thighs. He believed that she did ride horses in her spare time, but since they had started to work together she had not had much spare time.

She saw him in the mirror. "If you touch me," she said, "I shall puke."

"I never even thought of it," Leigh lied. "I've a full glass here, and a photograph. Both for you."

She turned, frowning. "Are you trying to be funny?" But she took the glass.

Leigh felt in his pocket, produced the snapshot. "It's not the slightest bit blue," he said. "But I would like you to study it, and tell me what you can about it."

He lay on the bed. He liked to watch her move, because, although she was not exactly a girl any more, she moved like a colt, throwing her legs in front of each other.

She came into the bedroom, the towel thrown over her left shoulder, the glass of champagne held in her right hand, the photograph in her left. She stopped moving about six feet from the bed, and her frown disappeared. "I have been thinking," she said. "We will have to give up. There is no one left, except. . . ."

"I never give up," Leigh said. "Although I agree we will *all* have to put our shoulders to the plough, this time." He smiled at her look of consternation. "It is becoming critical. But I have no intention of sacrificing any of us. Tell me about the photograph."

Carmel studied it. "Ibiza," she said. "That's where it is. I knew I recognised it, but for a moment I just couldn't place it." She raised her head. "Ibiza?"

"What's in a place?" Leigh asked. "They are all alike. Tell me what you see."

Carmel walked round the bed and sat on the other side. She held out her empty glass, and he filled it for her.

"Well," she said, draping her right knee over her left, "it's one of those poky little cafes which overflow on to the street down by the harbour; you can see the washing in the alley behind, and the unmade road."

"Go on."

"Well, there are people at the tables."

"Go on."

Her frown was back. "I'm not really on your wave length, right this minute. It looks a typical tourist shot to me. Do we know the tourist?"

"As a matter of fact, yes. But it's not her we are interested in. Tell me about the people."

She drank some champagne. "Well, there's the waiter. Looks a little lush to me. I suppose most of them are. Then there's an obvious honeymoon couple, mooning into each other's beer. Then there's a fat gentleman looking down the honeymoon wife's blouse. And then there's a drunk."

"And who would you say our tourist friend was trying to capture?"

Carmel finished her second glass of champagne. "Well," she said for the fourth time, "she seems to have managed to centre the drunk. I don't think she is a very good photographer."

"You may take it from me that she is a *very* good photographer, sweetheart," Leigh said. "So tell me about the drunk."

"Well," Carmel said, holding out her glass. "I suppose he's a fairly big man. It's difficult to be sure, when he's slouched over like that. But he has long legs."

"He's six feet two," Leigh agreed.

"And I shouldn't think he has been a drunk for too long," she said thoughtfully. "Even the way he's sitting, there doesn't seem to be any roll to his belly. That open shirt, too, you know, the chest underneath looks fairly hard."

"You may take my word for it," Leigh said. "Just about everything you can see or imagine about that fellow is fairly hard."

She did not rise to the bait. "But he isn't very young," she said. "I mean, he has the look of a forty plus. You know, the receding hair, isn't that a touch of grey at the temples? And he looks awfully run down. I mean, I know everyone in Ibiza looks a little run down, but that five-day growth, and the expression . . ."

"He is, at the moment, a little run down," Leigh agreed. "And he is also, as you so aptly put it, over forty. I believe he is a year younger than me."

"I didn't mean . . ."

"That he is in any way past it. He isn't. He may at this moment possess a permanent hangover, but hangovers can be cured, with suitable treatment. And even with a hangover, I imagine he could do you, or anyone else, a very nasty injury, if he wanted to."

Carmel's eyes came up. "You don't mean you want to use *him?* But what on earth . . . ?"

"You are looking at a very special him, sweetie," Leigh said. "For people in our position, you are looking at a dream come true. That is the most dangerous man in the world. Perhaps at this moment the operative word is 'was,' but we, or to be more precise *you,* are going to make it 'is' all over again."

Carmel's frown was back as she bent over the photo. "I'll have to take your word for it. But I don't really see what good he can do us. We have been employing quite a few of the world's most dangerous men, and women, over the past three years, and they haven't been able to get within shooting distance of our boy."

"Because they *had* to get within shooting distance. They can search this man until their hands drop off. They can investigate him and look inside his head and churn him around, and they won't find a thing. He doesn't use weapons."

"Yeah?"

"Hands only. I'm not quite sure how. You'll have to find that out. But I've heard of this character before. He used to work for the British. And the British have always had a lot of scores to settle, more than most since they have been unable to drop a hint that the Navy was on its way. So they took up using men like our drunk. And he was their best."

"And he'll work for us?"

"Seems he's fallen out with his masters, and retired. To what you see there. Jonquil spotted him. You remember Jonquil?"

"I don't like Jonquil."

"Well, cheer up, because I have a strong suspicion that Jonquil doesn't like you. But while she is officially working with us, she wants to get the best group together that she can, and she is an old acquaintance of this one. They worked together a few years ago and she learned then how good he is. So when she saw him in this cafe she took a snap and sent it along. Get him, she said, and our troubles are solved. Well, it occurred to me that she may be right, so long as we don't let her know what our particular trouble is. There's a dossier on him, which you might like to study. He really does provide all the answers. I've wired Jonquil to pick him up. But I'd like you to take over before they get to too much reminiscing."

"And won't he have to be told what we're at?"

Leigh smiled. "I don't think that will be necessary. I've been doing a lot of thinking about our situation. About our failures. It has occurred to me that we may have been a little too straightforward, up to now. We have seen the problem in only one dimension. I think, in trying to solve it, we have lost sight of our true objective. You don't play chess, so you wouldn't appreciate it, but there is a saying that the threat is far greater than the execution. Which really means that your opponent can become so obsessed by the threat, if it is real enough, that he can overlook everything else, and leave himself exposed to a very simple thrust. Think of this man as a threat."

Carmel looked at the photograph again. "A retired British agent, who kills only with his hands, and who you regard as the most dangerous man in the world," she said thoughtfully. "It sounds very interesting. And all I have to do is persuade him to work for us."

"Jonquil will do that. You just have to guide him in the right direction."

"That sounds even more interesting. What is this explosive character called?"

Leigh poured champagne. "His name is Wilde. Jonas Wilde."

ii

The city of Ibiza hides at the western end of a harbour concealed
by the promontory of Grossa. Behind this massive natural breakwater
the Ibizans have constructed one of their own, to make the harbour
a place of crowded peace, where even the strongest winds do little
more than ruffle the surface of the water. Like so many old Mediterranean towns, Ibiza itself is a citadel, perched on the top of its hill,
surrounded by massive walls which remain in a remarkable state of
repair. But of course it had long since overflowed into the wide
squares and tree-lined boulevards of a typical Spanish resort town,
on the one hand, and into a maze of little unmade alleys and seem-
ingly tottering brick houses by the waterfront. Only the cafes are common to both sides of the town, and the hippies. Ibiza is the mecca
of those young people who feel that, as life is at best a short and
precarious business, it had better be enjoyed, providing one can occasionally raise the price of a meal. For clothes, the barest necessity
will always do, and vagrancy, as it would be interpreted in North
America or Northern Europe, does not exist in the minds of the relaxed central Mediterranean.

"So how about it?" the girl asked. "I'll be good, man. You won't
have known anything better." The suggestion was faintly contemptu-
ous. "And all I'm asking is dinner. If it's a good dinner."

Wilde focussed with difficulty. He usually had trouble in focus-
sing, nowadays, but this was deliberate. Sharp images fell into one
of three, where females were concerned, and they were all calculated
to depress. Fuzzy images left him no more than nauseated. As fuzzy
images went, this girl wasn't bad. She was small, and dark, and
vaguely French. She wore a sheer blouse and a long skirt, which suggested that while she wanted to show off her rather small breasts
she was not so anxious to display her legs.

Dinner was unlikely to cost him more than five pounds, even with
the sort of liquor she would require. But how did she know, from
looking at him, that he possessed seven hundred pesetas to spare?

There was all the ingrained suspicion, the built up misanthropy,
bubbling away inside his brain. She was a human being, and Wilde
had known too many of those, too well, and too badly.

He felt in his pocket, took out a crumpled note. "So have a good dinner."

She frowned at him. "I'm not a whore, you know. Nor a beggar. I liked you."

"Past tense," Wilde agreed. "So why knock your luck?"

She hesitated. Her hand, starting to slide across the table, checked and slid back. She stood up. "You're pissed," she said. "I'm not a thief."

"Lady," Wilde said. "If I was pissed, I'd buy you that dinner personally. If I thought you could get me pissed, I'd buy you dinner *and* breakfast, and leave you fit only for a nunnery. I don't happen to believe in either of those possibilities."

"You fancy yourself."

"I don't fancy anyone else, that's for sure."

"So have fun." But the note was gone. And a moment later, so was she. Wilde leaned back and snapped his fingers, and the boy appeared beside his table.

"That jug," Wilde pointed out, "is empty."

"You wish another?" The boy seemed doubtful.

"How many have I had?"

"You have had five jugs, señor," the boy said.

"And you want me to stop on an odd number? *Malo, malo.*"

"It is bad, señor," the boy agreed. "Too much sangria, it affects the head. When it is hot."

"But you serve it cold." He felt like an argument.

"I mean the sun, señor." The boy's eyes lifted, and Wilde half turned his head. Another young man stood behind him. A very large young man.

"You wouldn't by any chance be throwing me out?"

"No, no, señor. But we think, maybe, it is time for siesta, you know, a nice sleep on the bed, and then, then, señor," he said, with the air of a knight who has spotted the Holy Grail, "then you can come back, and señor, there will be more sangria. Night-time is the time for sangria. You drink here until two, three in the morning, señor."

"Sangria is better, at night," said the giant, a rumble of distant thunder.

Now why the hell, Wilde thought, don't I tell them to get knotted? Because undoubtedly it will end with me in an Ibizan gaol, and he was not sure there was anyone around who would get him back out. But he had had five jugs of sangria, and as the young man no doubt feared, that was more than enough to make him a little bolshie.

He sighed, and stood up. The two young men looked concerned. Perhaps they had misjudged his size; even several months' dissipation had added little to the thirteen stones which were evenly distributed over his six feet two inches of height. Or perhaps they had not looked closely enough at the granite hardness of the lean face.

But the pale blue eyes remained reassuringly mild, and the voice was soft. "So I'm not wanted," he said. "No hard feelings, señor." He patted the boy on the shoulder, and thrust his right hand towards the giant.

"No hard feelings, señor," the giant agreed, and squeezed. And then began to suck air through his nostrils, loudly, while even the sun tan seemed to drain from his face.

Wilde forced the strength down his shoulder, exerting all the tremendous pressure that he had at his call. The giant sat down with a faint moan, and Wilde relaxed. He had not actually heard the crack, but he had felt something give. The giant's mouth sagged open as he stared at his hand, which had become withered. Tears rolled down his cheeks.

"Señor," cried the boy. "Señor? What have you done?"

"Squeezed," Wilde said. "I think he wants to have some plaster. I wouldn't want him hanging around when I come back. For some more sangria."

He stumbled down the steps and across the road. A car stopped abruptly and blew aggressively. Wilde reached the edge of the dock and gazed at the blue water, so clear he could see the myriad fish swimming just below the surface. And the water in Ibiza was a lot dirtier than most.

So he had been a vicious fool. Was he ever anything more than that, a vicious fool? Wasn't that the real reason he hadn't risked a shindig? Because the Spanish police, if they ever did get him inside, and start to check back, might not ever let him go again? And that went for almost every police force in the world.

He thrust his hands into his pockets, walked along the dock in the direction of the jetty. There the yachts were moored, stern on, and as he no longer had a yacht he could perhaps dream a little.

And there too was an upper walk, on which there were seats, and a view over the gulf and the sea beyond. A good place for a siesta.

Because the boy had been right. The ground was not behaving at all well, and neither were his legs, while his feet were being positively mutinous. One of his staggers took him sideways, almost into the street, and another car braked and blew. Wilde erected two fingers, and walked on. The jetty was only a few feet away. Now he had to be careful. A stagger the wrong way would land him in the drink. He hugged the wall, and two bikini-clad girls found their way round him, and looked over their shoulders, giggling.

So up them as well, he thought. Now he was passing the yachts. All kinds, from hundred-foot floating hotels to little sailing boats. *Regina B* would have looked good, moored with her stern to the dock in the midst of this lot, a true sailing ship, owned and sailed by a true sailor, dominating all the sea-going lounge lizards.

And if he were walking along here, knowing he was going back to *Regina B,* he wouldn't be hugging the wall, obviously pissed out of his mind. That would be nice.

But how could he ever go on board *Regina B* again? She carried too many ghosts. And one ghost in particular, which would be with him until the day he died. Of cirrhosis of the liver?

In any event, she wasn't there, and to the girls in their bikinis and the men in their briefs he was just a drunk, another drunk, an Ibiza drunk, harmless enough, so long as one didn't let him on board.

And now he was at the end of the jetty, standing by the lighthouse. Correction, leaning against the light tower to stop himself from falling over. From here the harbour was on his left, the new marina was in front of him, directly across the bay, and the sea was on his right, beyond the gulf. He had known this sea at its roughest; today it was at its quietest. A simply gorgeous Mediterranean afternoon. To be spent sleeping.

On the upper level? He regarded the steps. He wasn't really in the mood to count them; he wasn't sure that he would arrive at the same figure twice running. He was quite sure that there were far too many. And before he knew it he was sitting on the hot stone of the dock itself, his sandal-clad feet thrust out over the water. So what was more comfortable than this particular dock? Certainly not the seats above. And it was Ibiza. No one, least of all a policeman, was at all likely to come along and tell him to move. He could sit here and sleep away the rest of his life.

But maybe he was being optimistic. Because surely he hadn't been sitting here for more than a few minutes, and already someone *was* standing over him. Waiting for him to look up.

On the other hand, looking up wasn't exactly going to be a hardship. Without trying to he could focus on a pair of white high-heeled sandals, which contained a pair of small sun-tanned feet, out of which rose two narrow, equally brown, and equally attractive ankles, which debouched into long, slender legs which seemed to stretch for an interminable distance above him, before they reached the even more attractive wind-ruffled hem of a black and white vertical-striped short skirt. It was part of a suit, and the jacket was also black and white striped, but at the thighs the slenderness ended, as the waist dipped into an isthmus before flaring into a forty-inch bust line.

He could think of only one woman he had ever known with a figure as magnificently misproportioned as that. When that thought had sunk in, he hastily looked at her face. Her hair was genuine, a shade darker than carrot, long and wavily untidy. Her complexion was pale, spotted with large freckles. Her eyes were hazel, set wide apart to hover above the extreme corners of her generous mouth; surprisingly, the large tinted horn-rimmed spectacles behind which they sheltered increased their attractiveness. Her nose was a perfect small-scale model of the Cortina ski jump. She had a cleft in her chin, and dimples. She could easily have been assembled by a tired Deity at the end of a long day, from leftover parts. Wilde remembered that she even had good hands hidden inside her white gloves.

But he also remembered that she had nothing to do with God; rather the reverse.

He put his hands down and pushed, lost his balance and fell over.

The woman knelt beside him, held his arm. "I always knew," she said. "That the drink was going to get to you, one day."

Now he remembered her name as well. "Oh, God," he begged. "Jonquil Malone."

CHAPTER 2

"Do you think you can stand up, Jonas?" asked Jonquil Malone.

"Now, be honest," Wilde said. "Why should I want to stand up?"

"Because you can't spend the rest of your life sitting at the end of this dock. It might rain."

"It never rains, in Ibiza, in the summer."

"It's not summer yet," she pointed out. "Besides, I would like to have a talk with you."

"Take a seat."

She looked at the grey stone with considerable distaste. "I have a boat," she remarked. "You like boats, Jonas."

"I don't think boats like me."

"Didn't you use to live on one?"

"Almost all my life. I thought it was time for a change."

"My boat isn't far. You walked past it just now."

"And you thought I was going to commit suicide?"

"No," she said seriously. "I don't think you'd dare ever do that. There'd be too many people anxious to pull you in on the other side. Jonas, what do I have to do to get you to come and have a drink with me?"

"Mention the word drink, in the first place," he said. "And afterwards, let me have a nap with my head resting right there." He touched the top button of her blouse.

"Done."

"Now I know I have D.T.s."

She shrugged; while stooping in a slight breeze it was an entrancing operation, for the onlooker. "So maybe I liked you too, once. Come on, now, make an effort."

Wilde put his right hand down, and Jonquil took his left arm. He remembered that apart from using her ability as a contortionist as a cover, from time to time, she was also accomplished at other things, a very highly trained young woman who worked for . . . now there was a problem. He had never found that out. And the last time they had met . . .

He found himself standing up, leaning against the light tower. Jonquil was panting.

"The last time you and I were in close proximity," he pointed out. "You scuttled off and left me with three bullets in various parts of my anatomy."

"I didn't think they'd do any permanent damage, and I knew you were in good hands. And I was right, wasn't I?"

Wilde started to scratch his head, and also to fall over. She put her arm around his waist.

"There's a gangplank," she said a little anxiously. "Of course, the water isn't very deep . . ."

Wilde was concentrating on getting one foot in front of the other, and in not succumbing to her perfume or the temptation to look down to his right. "But it's also very salt and wet. Does your boat rise to a shower?"

"Two," she said. "Stop here."

He obeyed. Between himself and the harbour was a forty-foot motor cruiser; even to his fogged gaze he could recognise that she was a lot of ship, with a planing hull for a good turn of speed—she might be uncomfortable in rough weather, but in these sunlit waters it was usually possible to choose your day—with a stern cabin behind the enclosed wheelhouse, and a comfortable saloon forward, he figured, before one reached another sleeping cabin. Her name was *Esmeralda,* and she flew the red, white, and blue quarters of Panama.

"Well?" Jonquil asked.

"I'm a sailing man, myself."

"But she has a pair as well," Jonquil said, just a little acidly. "Diesels. Wouldn't you like to sleep with your head on them?"

"Sleep, no. I admit it'll be a toss-up as to which pair I'd rather play with."

"So help yourself on board," she said, and released him.

For a moment he swayed, while he stared at the narrow plank which connected the stern of the yacht with the dock. There was a rope grab rail, but beneath it there were several feet of opaque water.

"Bunty," Jonquil called.

A young man appeared from the wheelhouse. He was below medium height and heavily built; he reminded Wilde of a slightly undersized ox, and had a rather ox-like face. A hostile ox. Maybe a bull.

"Would you be a dear, Bunty, and help Mr. Wilde on board," Jonquil said.

"Your husband?" Wilde asked.

"My crew," Jonquil said.

"Hi," Wilde said. "I'm her favourite dead beat." He placed one foot on the plank and held out his hand. Bunty reached forward and jerked. Wilde shot across the plank before he quite realised where he was going, and landed on his hands and knees on the deck. "Ow."

"You're sure you know what we're doing?" Bunty asked.

"It's time you met that plane," Jonquil said. "I will guarantee that you won't recognise him when you get back. In which case, you had better pray that he won't recognise you, either. He can be a most unpleasant man."

"And you'll be all right?" Bunty asked.

"I have most-favoured-nation status," Jonquil said, and shook herself at him.

Wilde was hanging on to one of the deck stanchions, and clawing himself up. "Why the hell is this boat rocking?" he demanded.

"It's not used to your company. Come along, darling." She had her arm round his waist again and was gently urging him towards the wheelhouse door. Passers-by on the dock stopped to comment, and were removed by Bunty's beetle-like stare as he joined them.

The wheelhouse was a place of cool efficiency, with a drop-down table and some impressive instrumentation.

"You mean you actually use this thing?" Wilde asked.

"When I can find the time." She guided him towards the companion ladder leading aft.

Here indeed was a master stateroom, in which bunks had been replaced by a double bed. To the left was the bathroom.

"Sit down," Jonquil commanded.

Wilde sat on the lid of the toilet and gazed into the basin. "Are you going to wash my face?"

"Everything in its proper order. Open wide."

He obeyed, and a long finger suddenly entered his mouth. "If you bite me I shall not be pleased," she warned.

Wilde gagged as he tried to speak, and a moment later was being violently sick. Jonquil left him to it and departed, came back a moment later and switched on the cold tap. The water flowed on to his head and cascaded past his ears and cleaned out the basin all at once.

"I've put the kettle on," she said.

"You offered me a drink," Wilde spluttered.

"And I'm giving you a drink," she said. "Coffee and fruits salts." She switched off the water. "Now, if you can stand, I recommend a shower. Your clothes smell as if they've been slept in. Don't tell me," she added hastily. "They have been slept in. I'll put them in the gash, shall I?" She was undoing buttons and zips with tremendous efficiency.

Wilde leaned against the bulkhead. The yacht was still moving far too violently, but some of the constant swinging had gone from his head. A moment later the shower jet played on his face, and Jonquil hastily stepped back. "Don't fall down," she recommended.

The door closed. He discovered he was naked. In some mysterious fashion she had even removed his shoes. And the cold water felt so good. He just stood there, allowing it to splatter across his face and chest. Of course he had to think. One always had to think, about Jonquil Malone. And a man in his position had to think more deeply than most. He had not really figured on being recognised by anyone. Presumably it had to happen, sometime. But Jonquil Malone . . .

The door opened. "You seem to be asleep," she said. She had undressed, but looked as if she hadn't, almost; apparently she did not sunbathe in the nude.

"Hungry," he said. "I'm hungry."

"Everything in its proper place. I don't like wasting food." She was soaping, again with tremendous speed and efficiency.

"Ever been a nurse?"

"The people I work for expect everyone to be everything, from time to time." She took the shower head from its bracket and rinsed him. "Are you capable of drying yourself? I hear the kettle."

He rubbed thoughtfully, gazed through the open door at the bed. He could sleep on that bed. And when he awoke he would feel a whole lot more like coping with the situation. But with Jonquil around would he ever awake?

She had put on a bathrobe to negotiate the wheelhouse on the way to the galley; now she returned with a cup of coffee in one hand and a full pot in the other. "Drink it up."

He sipped, and shuddered, and sat on the bed.

"How do you feel? You're looking better. A little more alert to the fact that you're in a cabin with a beautiful woman."

"You were telling me about your employers," Wilde said.

Jonquil placed the kettle on a rubber mat on the dressing table, leaned against the bulkhead, and folded her arms. "I think you should tell me about yours, first. Would you like to borrow a razor?"

Wilde finished his coffee, and she refilled the cup. "Everything in its proper place," he said.

She sighed. "I was thinking of your pillows. So what happened?"

"I got fed up," Wilde said.

"Because Catherine Light was killed?"

Wilde drank some more coffee. "You do make the most alarming remarks, Jonquil."

"Meaning I shouldn't know anything about Lady Light? Or about anything else? I know a great deal about you, Jonas. Almost as much as anybody else in the world. Try this for size. You worked for British Intelligence for something like twenty years, principally as their hatchet man. You're a great pal of Coolidge Lucinda, of the CIA. Well, I learned that in your company, didn't I? Your boss is, or was, Sir Gerald Light, baronet, who controls the peacetime Special Operations Executive, and specifically the Elimination Section. It was he who gave you your code name, Eliminator. And over the past few years you have been showing a lot of interest in Sir Gerald's so beautiful young wife, Cathy."

"You know," Wilde said. "As you and I are alone on this tub, you really are sticking your neck out."

"It's my job," she said. "And then, only a few months ago, Cathy Light stopped a bullet right where it would do her looks most harm. That's my figuring, anyway. So the papers said she died of a sudden heart attack. Cathy Light? She was as thin as a rake and in good shape, I'd say, from her photographs. And almost as soon as she is decently interred the Eliminator ups and quits. That's the word we have, anyway."

"We?" Wilde asked.

"So you took off and went on a monumental bender," Jonquil said. "From which I have just rescued you."

"I wonder why," Wilde said.

"You are a valuable article, Jonas. Add up all the thousands of pounds Her Majesty's Government spent on training you. Start thinking of all the governments who would like to catch hold of you, either to execute, to interrogate, or to employ."

"Only you happen to know more than most," Wilde said. "You happen to know what I look like."

"I also happen to know your habits," Jonquil said. "We talked, remember, last time we were shacked up together. You have never actually killed a man in Spain. Or a woman. So you feel safe here. I have a good memory."

Wilde lay down on the bed. "You made me a promise."

"You're not yet ready to go to sleep," she said. "I'd like to know, have you quit? Or is it only a bender?"

"I was going to make up my mind when I woke up."

Jonquil took off her bathrobe and came across the cabin. She crawled on to the bed and remained kneeling, just out of reach. She might have been posing for a calendar.

"And I woke you up too soon?" she asked. "I think it's time you did quit, Jonas. I don't think you enjoy killing people any more. At least, not all by yourself."

"And you think it would feel better in your company?"

"We worked pretty well once before."

He seized her arm, drew her forward on to her belly beside him. "You have the happy knack of seeing only what you want to see. What about those bullets?"

"You don't still have them in you?" she asked innocently.

"If you look closely, you can spot where they came out. Do you know, I had supposed that everything that has happened recently had put me off women but good."

"And it hasn't?" She eased herself on to her elbows, kissed him on the mouth, and then took off her glasses. "I'm glad of that. We never really had a chance to get together, last time, did we?" She smiled. "Except for that hilarious episode in the bathroom."

He corrected his previous mistake. She was one of the few women he had met about whom he was genuinely curious, no doubt because she claimed to be a contortionist. So this had been her cover at the time of their first meeting, but there was certainly a lissomeness, an extremely healthy muscularity, about her which had been fascinating his memory for years. Nor did she disappoint him in the flesh. He had supposed, having a suspicious nature, that her deliberate titillation had been all directed towards blanketing his mind, but now it occurred to him that she might have been intending to satisfy a curiosity of her own as well.

She sighed, and blew into his ear at the same time. "I'm glad I caught you before the final decay set in."

"Do you think you could let me go, now?" Wilde asked. "You may not have cramp from this position, but I am starting to develop a twinge."

"Sorry."

He took another shower. This one he could appreciate more.

Wilde towelled, closed the bathroom door behind him, and hated himself. And also wondered why. He was out. He might not be prepared to admit it to anyone else, but it was a decision he had taken the moment he had seen the blood dribbling from Cathy Light's chest. He was out for a lot of reasons. Not merely because he was tired and therefore vulnerable. Not merely because he could rate himself as what he was, a cold-blooded killer whose flashes of humanity or humor only illustrated the darkness that lay between. Not merely because he no longer knew if he could summon the tremendous concentration which had been his stock in trade for so many years, and which had been responsible for his own survival as it had also been responsible for so many deaths. But because he had a habit of falling in love, and causing women to fall in love with him; and everyone who had was now dead. He exuded destruction like an aroma; those who could not reach Wilde reached his woman.

So he would not ever again be involved. So what was he thinking of, as he gazed at the red-headed woman who had broken his cover. Except that he did not any longer have a cover.

Only it was ingrained so deeply in his subconscious that a broken cover meant death, either for himself or for the transgressor, he could no longer shake it off. And it still applied, there was the rub. For the people she worked for, the people who had sent her to find him, might have methods of questioning with which he could not cope, methods of brainwashing which would get past even his guard, to infiltrate the system he had just abandoned, or even to turn him against it.

And knowing that, what alternatives did he have?

Jonquil Malone sat up. "You don't look very pleased."

"I am now sober," Wilde pointed out. "It was your idea."

"I read somewhere that drunk men aren't very good at anything."

"It's a point." He sat beside her. "I'd like you to know that I don't bear a grudge for the way you wandered off and left me playing hide-and-seek with an army."

"I've explained about that one," she said. "Really. And you want to remember that they roughed me up a little first. But I just couldn't get involved with the CIA and all of that. My people like to work very much on their own."

"Your people," Wilde said. "You never did get around to telling me who they were."

"Well, I'm about to," she said.

"Eh?" She had taken him by surprise.

And now his preoccupation had taken her by surprise. Her eyes widened.

"For God's sake, Jonas, you weren't thinking of . . . you were. Me? And after the best five minutes you've had in your life?"

"A debatable point," Wilde said. "I am at least fifteen years older than you, and therefore have had a good many more."

"You are sixteen years older than me," she said. "I was on my very first assignment when we met last. And I wouldn't like to bet on your figures."

"You," Wilde said. "Talk too much. Which is one of the problems I have in mind."

"And how would you do it?" she asked. "Would you hit me, Jonas? But I should be standing up, shouldn't I? Then would you squeeze the life from me?" She took his hands and placed them on her throat. "You could do it now, couldn't you? And then just walk off the ship, and nobody would ever even know you'd been here. Save Bunty."

He tightened his fingers, just a little, and her eyes widened, just a little.

"Or you could hold my head in a bucket of water," she said. "There's a bucket in the after locker. I promise you I won't move, while you go and get it."

Wilde released her. "You are a very funny girl, Jonquil. Come to think of it, you always were. Now why don't you tell me what this is all about?"

"I don't think I will," she said. "Then you'll have to torture me. I'll bet you're good at that, Jonas. I think you're a sadist, at heart."

"Don't I have to be, to commit murder?"

"You're not a murderer. You were proud of that, once. You're an executioner. That's different. It is possible for you to hate your work. Do you hate your work?"

"I'm no longer working."

"Then why have you got another hard-on? You really got yourself worked up over throttling me."

Wilde sighed. Being in her company was rather like being stuck on a perpetual roller coaster. "I didn't mean to throttle you, Jonquil. I got the impression that you were enjoying yourself."

"I like to feel your hands."

"So my hands like to feel you. Which should explain all physical variations. But much as I like you, Jonquil, and I really do, I am going to get very angry if you don't tell me why you came looking for me, and who sent you to do that, and just how you found me. I would also like to know how you know so much about my business. I seem to remember that you found it rather easy to locate me the last time we ran into each other."

"Oh, we have our little ways. Do you know, Jonas, I have never seen you angry? I thought that a man in your position couldn't afford to get angry."

"You keep forgetting that I am no longer in that position," Wilde reminded her. "I can get as angry as I like."

"Show me," she smiled.

Wilde seized her arm, rolled her across the bed and across his lap at the same time, and slapped her as hard as he could across the buttocks.

"Jesus Christ," she howled, and wriggled forward.

Wilde retained his grip on her arm, and as he raised his hand again she gave another yelp and twisted on her back.

"I'm in agony," she grumbled. "I don't think you've gone off at all."

"Well, you deserved it," he pointed out. "Firstly for breaking into my little drunken idyll, and secondly for supposing that I would ever consider working for the IRA, or any of your peculiar Irish political armies. Now, tell me what you did with my clothes and I'll depart."

She sat up, apparently having forgotten about the slap. "I don't work for the IRA, Jonas."

"So here we go again." Wilde sighed. "You take orders, sweetheart. You were taking them the first time we met, and you are still taking them now. Supposing they don't arise in either Dublin or Belfast, just where do you go to collect your pay?"

"I go to Tel Aviv," she said.

ii

Wilde sat down again, slowly, on the bed beside her. "You expect me to believe that you are a long-legged Jewish mick? Oh, come now."

Jonquil looked positively sulky, and she didn't have the face for it. "I don't see why not. I spent a lot of my girlhood on a kibbutz. My husband worked there." She stuck her glasses back on her nose.

"And his name was Malone?"

"Of course not. That is my maiden name."

"And the poor old sod got killed fighting gloriously against ten thousand Arabs, and in revenge you decided to do your bit."

"Don't you *like* the Jews, Jonas?"

"A lot of the time I don't like anybody, sweetheart. Not even you. As a matter of fact, I have the highest possible respect for the Jews. But not quite to the extent of working for them. And certainly not to the extent of killing for them. In case you have missed the point of much of what I have said and you claim to have observed, I have retired."

"Nobody said anything about killing anybody, Jonas. And Peter didn't die in battle; he was overweight and died of a heart attack. He was a few years older than me. And by that time I had already been enrolled in this particular business. Tel Aviv needs all the good undercover agents it can get."

"I read the papers, from time to time. You never kill anyone intentionally, is that it? Just if they get between you and your target?"

"Those days are done, Jonas. Oh, perhaps that sort of thing was necessary once. But not now. Now it is all sorted out, at least officially. But there are still a few anarchistic people around, and we are sitting targets. We need good people in the important places. Some of them more surprising than you may think."

She was sitting up again, and leaning forward, and the annoyance had gone from her face. She was a magnificent sight.

"You mean I'd spend the rest of my life sitting next to the stewardess just in case someone suggested there was a bomb on board? There aren't that many pretty stewardesses in the world, Jonquil, much less in El-Al alone."

"A man like you," she said dreamily, "with your experience and your peculiar talents, would have more important things to do than guard planes against hijacks. And it would be something worthwhile, Jonas. Something constructive. You can't hate the world that much. Even if you do, here's your chance to expiate some of that hate. And what makes you think you *can* retire? The word has gone out, you know, Jonas. Wilde has quit. Wilde has walked away from his security blanket. Have you ever sat back to think just how many people will be interested in that message, and just how many people can recognise you as easily as I did? You can't hide forever, and if you go on drinking you are going to be that much more vulnerable to the person who eventually catches up with you. I always had an idea that skill alone could never have kept you alive; I figured you'd also need a whole hell of a lot of luck. And I think this last week proves me right, that of everyone who might want to lay hands on Jonas Wilde, I was the first actually to spot him."

She paused, for breath. But there was no arguing with the terrible good sense she had just delivered.

"And presumably," he said, "I would also be working for you."

"I would certainly try to make sure that we worked together as often as possible. But even I have superiors."

"Now that really does surprise me."

She ignored the sarcasm. "As a matter of fact, Bunty has just gone to meet our current superior, and they will be back here any minute. That could be them now."

An engine was muttering on the dock behind the ketch.

"Does he like to interview his prospective candidates in the nude too?"

"*She* will just love to interview you in the nude, Jonas. So use the towel. That kind of competition I can do without."

The yacht swayed as someone crossed the gangplank, and they heard footsteps on the deck overhead. Jonquil got out of bed and pulled on her bathrobe. Wilde wrapped the towel round his waist, and turned to look at the companionway.

The woman was tall and very fair; her hair was shoulder length in a fine gold, and curled at the ends. She looked younger than Jonquil, which did not altogether surprise Wilde; he had been discovering over the past few years that his employers as well as his adversaries had been growing younger and younger. Her face was a trifle long but beautifully proportioned, with a straight nose and a somewhat small mouth above a pointed chin. Her eyes were wide set and deep blue. She was not, he supposed, beautiful, but this was perhaps because she was so very serious. It was certainly an interesting face, suggesting all manner of unusual facets beneath the coldness of the exterior, and the coldness itself was a considerable challenge.

And there wasn't a great deal wrong with her body. Her torso was bare except for the halter bra of what was probably a bikini, and the strap of a large bag which hung from her shoulder. Her breasts naturally could not compare with Jonquil's, but they were quite large enough to fill a man's hands with something to spare, he figured, and she had a nice flat belly. Her legs were lost beneath the long pale blue skirt which reached her flipflops. But he did not really fear disappointment down there, either. Whenever she chose to reveal them.

"Good afternoon, Jonquil," she said. "I see you have already introduced yourself to Mr. Wilde."

"We're old friends, remember?" Jonquil asked. "Jonas, this is Carmel Wane."

"My pleasure. Jonquil tells me you're her boss."

Carmel Wane glanced at Jonquil, and then allowed her eyes to return to Wilde, face and body. It was a remarkably steady gaze; he did not think it was missing a mole.

"On this particular assignment, yes," she said, and stepped forward, close to him. She placed her hand on his left breast and slowly closed her fingers. Wilde deliberately remained relaxed, but her expression did not change. She released him and did the same at his belly, sliding her fingers into the top of the towel before squeezing.

"How long have you been on the booze?" she asked.

"A few weeks," Wilde said.

"You will have to give it up."

"Sorry, Miss Wane. My habits are my own."

She released him again and stepped back. "Because you always deliver the correct result. Is that it?"

"It's not much of a claim, although it's all I have," he said. "But I'm retired."

"From killing. Jonquil has told me." She glanced around the cabin with an expression of disgust. "This place smells of sweat, semen, and stale alcohol. Do you possess any clothes, Mr. Wilde?"

"You'd better ask Jonquil."

"At this moment, he does not," she said. "Don't you have any clothes anywhere, Jonas?"

"I've a room," he said.

"Would that be the key I took from your pocket?"

"I suppose it must be."

"Bunty," Jonquil said. "Would you go and empty Mr. Wilde's room and bring everything you can find down here."

Bunty nodded, and returned on deck.

"You mean I'm staying?" Wilde asked.

"I had thought you were quite comfortable here," Carmel Wane said, once more allowing her gaze to settle on Jonquil as she might have inspected a peculiarly repulsive beetle. "Is there somewhere else we can go, without being overlooked by the people on the dock?"

"There's a saloon, forward of the wheelhouse."

"Then let us go there. Put some clothes on, Jonquil. I'm sure Mr. Wilde has had enough excitement for one afternoon. And then we shall all have tea."

"Tea?" Wilde inquired.

"It is an old English custom," Carmel Wane pointed out. "My mother always took tea at four o'clock in the afternoon." She climbed the steps to the wheelhouse. "Jonquil tells me you know about boats."

"I like them."

She glanced at him. "So tell me about this one, Mr. Wilde."

"She's fast."

"I meant, display your knowledge to me."

"Ah. Well, she's a planing motor boat." He paused.

"What is a planing motor boat?"

"It means she has a shallow, V-shaped hull design, which allows her to sit *on* the water rather than in it."

"Then it is possible to have another arrangement?"

"Of course. The traditional design of a motor boat is with a displacement hull, which means that the ship will sit deeply in the water and go through it rather than across it."

"Why should you have one or other of any of those?"

"It depends on what you want to use the boat for. A displacement hull, properly handled, will take the worst weather safely. But she will never be very fast. This boat wouldn't really want to be caught out in a gale, but she has the speed to run away from strong winds."

"I see." Carmel Wane stood at the wheel, rested her hands on the spokes, and peered at the windshield in front of her. "What is that round thing?"

"It's called a Clearview Screen. It's a separate piece of glass set into the glass of the windshield itself, and worked by an electric motor, so that when it is turned on it whirls at a tremendous speed, with the result that any water settling on it is thrown off again and it remains clear all the time. Whereas normal windshield wipers can't cope with big seas and really heavy rain, if you happen to be trying to find a landmark or pick up a buoy."

"But isn't that a radar screen over there?"

"Looks like it," Wilde said. "And very nice, too. But there are still occasions when a helmsman has to make a visual identification."

She nodded thoughtfully. "Now, these handles above me? That is a light, is it not?"

"A searchlight, yes."

"But this one . . ." She frowned.

"It's called the D.F. Stands for direction finding aerial. If you stick your head out of the door, you'll see, on top of the coach roof, a large loop aerial. And dotted all over the shores of the Mediterranean, and all other seas, are radio beacons which emanate a steady morse signal, usually the first letters of the name of the station itself. So if you tune your radio to the correct wave length, you will hear the signals beaming towards you, and by turning the loop . . ."

"Of course," she said. "Until the signal is at its loudest, you know you are somewhere along that bearing."

"No," Wilde said. "You turn the loop until the signal fades altogether, and you know you are somewhere along *that* bearing. Because when the aerial is pointing directly at the station it cannot pick it up. It's called the null."

"And by taking two of those, and observing exactly where they cross, it's possible to obtain one's position at sea," she said.

"It's safer to take three," Wilde said. "As I think you know, Miss Wane. Do you consider *I* know anything about boats?"

"I'm sure you're an expert, Mr. Wilde." She turned away from the helm and went down the ladder to the saloon. "But unfortunately I am not considering employing you as a crew for this yacht. Suppose you wished to kill me, with your bare hands, how would you go about it?"

"I'd strangle you," Wilde said.

"And you have very strong fingers." She sat down on the U-shaped dinette, crossed her knees. "Do you have a cigarette?"

"Not in this towel."

Jonquil joined them; she had put on jeans and a mutton-cloth blouse, but left her feet bare. Her hair floated as she moved. She placed a packet of cigarettes and a gold lighter on the table, filled the kettle.

"Well trained," Wilde remarked.

"I like all my operatives to be well trained," Carmel Wane agreed. "And to know where the authority lies. I think you deliberately misunderstood me, just now, Mr. Wilde. Me, you could very probably strangle. Or you think you could. Suppose I was a man as strong as yourself, and the job had to be done very quickly and silently."

Wilde sat beside her. "That is a trade secret, Miss Wane. In any event, it is buried now."

"I would like to know, Mr. Wilde. It might even help me to convince myself that Jonquil has found the right man."

Jonquil turned back from the stove. "One doesn't make mistakes with characters like Wilde."

"I don't think he looks very deadly," Carmel Wane said. "Oh, I am sure he is very good in bed. He has the look of that." Once again she allowed her gaze to wander, rather distastefully. "But then, I am not employing him to go to bed with me, either. I was told you possess a special gift, Mr. Wilde. If you won't reveal it to me, then I'm afraid I do not see how we can work together."

"Neither can I," Wilde agreed. "When Bunty comes back with my clothes, I'll leave."

"Oh, I don't see how we could permit that either," Carmel Wane said. "Not after Jonquil has told you who we are."

Her gaze was remarkably steady, and her hands were remarkably visible, resting on the table. Her bag continued to hang from her shoulder. And yet Wilde could not really doubt that she also possessed a special gift, or she wouldn't be in this business at all.

And Jonquil, presently placing tea bags in little china teacups, which looked hideously inappropriate on a yacht like this, certainly possessed a special gift, of not being there when she was wanted, and of always being there when she wasn't wanted. At least as regards him. No doubt for Carmel Wane the reverse would obtain. And because he had recently made her very happy did not mean that she would refrain from sticking a knife between his shoulder blades. Besides, he wasn't sure that he had made her *very* happy; she was a good actress. "So I'm outnumbered," he agreed.

Jonquil stirred the tea bags. "Do be co-operative, Jonas darling. Carmel can really be quite nice."

Wilde smiled at the blond woman. "I'm sure you can, Miss Wane. If you must know, I made a study of anatomy when I first got into this business, I mean the one I have just left. I got together with a doctor friend of mine and asked him what was the quickest and surest way to end life, absolutely silently and without using weapons, and incidentally, with a total absence of pain. And he pointed out that a properly conducted judicial hanging is as good a way as any. As you know, the knot is placed just under the victim's ear. This is so, as the trap is sprung, all his weight pulls on the rope, and the knot acts as a sledge-hammer against a portion of his brain called the occidental process. This is a wad of muscle guarding the medulla, and the medulla, as you must also know, is that little knob-like mass of nerve ends which controls all of our unconscious processes, heartbeat, breathing, digestion, and so on. So, the knot presses against the occidental process with all the weight of a man's body, and the occidental process is driven into the medulla with that amount of force, and the medulla ceases to function, and everything else ceases to function as well. Death is instantaneous. The victim will not make a sound, because all of his ability to do so has been ended. He will feel nothing, because all his nerves have been cut off at the same instant. Nor will there immediately be any marks to reveal a cause of death, although of course a cursory medical examination will reveal the bruise behind his left ear."

"But you don't walk around with a rope and a convenient tree," Carmel Wane said.

"I taught myself how to replace the knot with the edge of my hand," Wilde said. "It is essentially a karate blow, but it is not a chop. That moves a short distance, and is delivered with the full force of the mind, supported by the arm. The mind is just as important in my blow, but it must also contain the full weight of my body, and it is generally delivered with the arm outflung to full length, the edge of the hand being aimed to connect just behind the ear, where the hangman's knot would be placed."

"It must have taken a great deal of practice."

"It did."

"And it must require a great deal of concentration."

"It does. The technique of the blow is the same as that of a really good boxer, the ability to transmit the full fighting weight into the fist as the decisive punch is delivered. That needs fitness and timing, more than anything else."

"Yes," she observed, once again scanning his body. "And of course, being able to deliver this blow allowed you to enter the presence of anyone without being searched, or in fact, after being searched to anyone's satisfaction. As you carried nothing which could remotely be considered a weapon. In fact, Mr. Wilde, you could have been stripped as naked as you are now, and still be as lethal as ever."

"That was the general idea," Wilde said.

"But he's given it up," Jonquil said, placing the cups of tea in front of them.

Carmel Wane did not appear to be listening to her. "On the other hand, Mr. Wilde, this method of yours depends on your being able to get right up to the person you are going to execute. And presumably, away again afterwards. I would have thought this also required a very special technique."

"It required a great deal of planning, and a very good back-up team, to be in the right place at the right time whenever I needed that much help, and yet never appear to be involved."

"And this you had."

"It was a good team," Wilde said a trifle sadly. "At least down to seven years ago."

"Then you were infiltrated by the Russians. Yes, Jonquil has told me about that. But still, for seven years you have been operating on your own. I think you have an unbecoming modesty, Mr. Wilde."

"Let's say it was too strenuous to last, which is why I've quit." Wilde drank tea, and shuddered. "Now, Miss Wane, I have been far too frank with you. I think you could be frank with me, in exchange."

"I thought Jonquil had already been frank with you. If you have indeed quit British Intelligence, there is a place for you in my organisation."

"You mean Israeli Intelligence?"

Carmel Wane glanced at Jonquil, and Jonquil returned her gaze without changing expression.

"We are a branch of Israeli Intelligence, yes, Mr. Wilde. Concerned with various specific projects, not all of which are obvious to the casual observer."

"And you run this special branch?"

"I am the present executive officer, Mr. Wilde. We have a superior. No doubt you will meet him in due course."

"And what are you presently engaged upon?"

Carmel Wane's mouth widened into what might easily have been mistaken for a smile. "You may not believe this, Mr. Wilde, but our present objective is to preserve a life which would appear to be very much in danger, and whose existence is vital to the very existence of Israel. But unfortunately the gentleman in question must not be aware that we are protecting him, as he would resent our attention. Which makes the whole thing very complicated. Tell me, have you ever heard of the state of Xanda?"

CHAPTER 3

Wilde drank tea, and considered. "Xanda is a small sheikdom some-where in the bottom half of the Arabian peninsula. For God knows how long it has been so poor that no one has ever wanted to do more than mark its existence on a map. But four years ago they struck oil. Actual drilling has only recently started, but I believe it is claimed to be the richest deposit ever found."

"Enough to supply all, just for example, of America's daily needs for fifty years," Jonquil Malone said.

"If those figures are accurate," Wilde said, "it does sound rather like a dream."

"They are accurate," Carmel Wane said. "It would appear that Xanda is actually sitting on top of a subterranean lake composed of nothing but oil. In ten years time it will be the richest country in the world. But that does not concern us, except that we hope to see it happen. Walid ben Ali, the Prince of Xanda—he will no longer permit anyone to call him the Sheikh—has suddenly become the most important man in the Middle East. But what is even more important, he is a friend of the Americans and all that the Americans stand for, and he has no wish ever to go to war with the Israelis. He only wishes to sell his oil, and to improve the conditions of his people, and personally to enjoy his sudden wealth."

"So bully for him," Wilde said.

"You make a very good cup of tea, Jonquil," Carmel Wane said. "I will have another. I agree with you, Mr. Wilde. But you can imag-ine that he is not the most popular man around, at this moment. He is upsetting his Arab neighbours; as they for centuries ignored Xanda's very existence, much less contributed anything to the solving of the various problems suffered by his father and himself, he sees no reason blindly to follow them now. Thus his very independent attitude. Then he also upsets the Russians, who regard themselves as the natural protectors of the Arabs. All the Arabs. And of course, more than any other, he upsets the various guerrilla organisations, who see in him nothing better than a traitor to the Arab cause."

"That figures," Wilde said.

"Thus there have been, and I am afraid there will continue to be, groups in opposition to him who will stop at nothing. For they too have a goal. Should the Prince die, Xandan policy may well change. In fact it is almost certain to do so. He has a son, but the child is only six. He is at school in England. So there would have to be a regency, and it is well known that not all of the Prince's closest advisers, and certainly not every member of his family, agree with his point of view. There have already been attempts on his life."

"I read of one, only recently," Wilde said. "Two girls and a man attempted to blow up his car. They failed. I gather that people who attempt such things always do fail, with the Prince of Xanda."

"They were garrotted, in public." Jonquil stirred tea with a faint shudder. "He may wish to become civilised, but he hasn't made it yet."

"It is our business to see that he lives long enough to do so," Carmel said. "I agree that as a rule he is very well protected. It is impossible to approach him without being searched. This goes not only for his officials, but any other officials, from whatever country, and even for his wives and concubines. Every morsel of food that passes his lips is pretasted. He is surrounded at all times by guards and bullet-proof materials. Unfortunately, we have observed a disturbing tendency in the past few months. As every attempt on his life has been discovered and punished, the Prince and his guards are becoming a trifle overconfident. Some of their precautions are being relaxed. Not very noticeably, perhaps. But we have noticed it, and so will other people. And the people who wish him dead are not going to give up. They have already sacrificed several operatives. They will be prepared to sacrifice quite a few more. And one day they will get through. Because the Prince is operating in the dark. He knows there are a lot of people who would happily see him buried. But he does not know who they are or where they come from. He does not realise that they are all part of a concerted effort, all aimed at ending his life."

"Unless we stop them," Jonquil said.

"I won't have any more tea, thank you," Wilde said. "It might make me go all woozy again. I hate to admit I'm a dumb bunny, but where do you lot come in? Supposing you are not the people aiming to kill him."

"Kill him?" Carmel demanded. "For God's sake." She got up, moved restlessly around the saloon. "He is our only friend in the Arab world. He is a balancing factor which takes care of our future no matter what events may conspire to change circumstances in the Middle East. He is our insurance policy. At all costs we must keep him alive. That is the first priority. But we realise that to do that involves another. We must find out exactly who are the members of this group dedicated to his destruction, and who is employing them, while at the same time making sure they do not succeed. To accomplish this, our special assignment group is hard at work all over the world, not only in the Middle East. But frankly, Mr. Wilde, the situation has taken a sudden turn for the worse. The Prince does not only want his people to prosper, he has every intention of prospering himself. Our agents have discovered that he has recently bought himself a yacht, to which he intends to retire, incognito, whenever he feels tired of garrotting people. In our opinion the risk involved in such an idea is unacceptable. Imagine, a man as vulnerable as that sailing around the Mediterranean with no more than a handful of guards. Think of the number of things which can go wrong with a boat? And if we have found out that this Mr. Watt is really Walid of Xanda, so can others. We want someone on board that boat who knows more than anyone else about keeping people alive."

"You have got hold of the wrong end of the stick."

"What about the old saying, set a thief to catch a thief?" Jonquil smiled.

"That is true, Mr. Wilde. Having murdered so many people in your time . . ."

"Uh-uh, Carmel," Jonquil said. "That is not a word we use. Jonas has *eliminated* the odd person from time to time."

Carmel Wane allowed herself a frosty smile. "Having eliminated so many people in your time, Mr. Wilde, you must be familiar with every possible means than can be used."

"And you see, Jonas," Jonquil said. "You are the only useful person we can send. Our agents, like me, are trained to defend themselves, and others, with weapons. But no one except his own special bodyguard is allowed to carry arms close to the Prince, so any attempt to infiltrate a normal agent to look after him would be useless. But you are just as effective without weapons as with them. You are the answer to a prayer. And then, you know about boats and the sea. You could spot much quicker than most if something was going wrong."

"You are also, judging by the facts given in your file," Carmel said, "the possessor of an acute and penetrating brain. You will serve, close to the Prince, and you will watch, and listen, and see. Because there can be no doubt that someone very close to him is masterminding these attempts on his life. I wish you to find out who."

"And you have no ideas?"

"Of course we have ideas, Mr. Wilde. But we are not going to tell you what we think. We would prefer an unprejudiced judgement."

"So what do I do? Walk up the Xandan royal palace and ask for a job?"

"I don't think you would be admitted. In fact, it is very likely that you would be shot. No, when we decided to employ you, Mr. Wilde, it was, as Jonquil has told you, with his yacht in mind. When I say yacht, I am speaking figuratively, of course. This ship is more than a hundred feet long and cost a quarter of a million pounds, which is actually peanuts to Walid at this moment. She is now in St. Tropez completing her fitting out, and he plans to join her for her maiden voyage under his ownership. Her captain is Spanish, but her crew are really all members of the Xandan secret police. There are, however, one or two posts which are to go to outsiders. One of them is head barman."

"Come again?"

"She means steward," Jonquil said. "We thought that might suit you rather well, Jonas. Providing you can keep yourself sober."

"According to your file, Mr. Wilde," Carmel Wane pointed out, "one of your hobbies is making cocktails, and mixing drinks, and things like that."

"Once upon a time," Wilde agreed, "before life became serious."

"Then I am sure you will welcome the opportunity to try your hand again. The important thing is that you are not a novice with whatever you are likely to find in the Prince's bar."

"I'll tell you a little secret," Wilde said. "I won't find anything in the Prince's bar, because presumably he doesn't drink."

This time Carmel's smile was more genuine. "I'm sure you'll find something there, Mr. Wilde. I told you, the Prince of Xanda does not hold entirely orthodox views, on religion any more than on politics."

"In which case, Miss Wane, he will be looking for a real expert."

"*He* won't be looking for anything. It is not something that he will personally attend to. But we have certain friends in his entourage, and they agree with our points of view and will indeed welcome our help in this matter. You will get the job, I promise you. You have already applied and are to be interviewed at the end of next week. For the next week, therefore, you will spend your time getting absolutely fit again. There is a little island off the southern tip of Majorca, called Cabrera. It is garrisoned by the Spanish Army, I believe, but in any event visitors are forbidden to land without permission, and we do not have such permission. But the authorities have no objection to it being used by visiting yachts; it really is, you see, just one enormous harbour. Jonquil and Bunty, with some help from you, I am sure, will take this boat over there and remain for a week, in which time they will get you into the best possible shape. At the end of that time they will take you across to St. Tropez, and in due course you will appear for your interview on board the *Female Spirit*. That is the name of the Prince's yacht."

"I thought it might be," Wilde agreed. "And when I do that, will I get the job?"

"You may count on it. Of course, you will have to be efficient and co-operative. You do understand that? The Prince likes them obsequious, and so do most of his entourage."

"I'll obseque to the best of my ability, supposing I take the assignment. I'm still trying to be quite sure what you want. Once on board, you would like me, firstly, to keep an eye open for any suspicious characters, and secondly, to see if I can discover which of the Prince's immediate pals is a rotten orange."

"Put very broadly, yes."

"And what do I do when I see a torpedo heading for the yacht?"

"You look after the Prince. But you won't see a torpedo, Mr. Wilde. It is not sufficiently accurate, the idea of using a submarine is too costly and too technically difficult for a guerrilla group, and it would be too public a confession of guilt for any nation. No, no, you are looking for something far more limited."

"And supposing I do discover something? How do I get back to you?"

"Oh, you won't be alone, Mr. Wilde," Carmel said. "We wouldn't do that to you. Nor, to be honest, would we be prepared to trust you to that extent. No, no, no, the application has been made in the names of Mr. and Mrs. Rupert Smart."

"Rupert?" Wilde inquired.

"Rupert," Jonquil said.

"It is entirely natural for a husband and wife team to take on the duties of running the domestic side of a large yacht. You have here a most impressive list of references." She opened her bag and took out a sheaf of papers and letters. "Don't you remember, Mr. Wilde, that you were *maître d'hôtel* and your wife was housekeeper at Claridge's once?"

"There have been so many," Wilde said. "One does tend to forget the smaller places. I tell you who I have forgotten though. My wife."

Carmel smiled at Jonquil, and Wilde found himself staring in the same direction. "No," he said. "I refuse to believe it."

"But she selected you herself, Mr. Wilde." Carmel had resumed her rummaging. "Two passports, one wedding certificate, a set of photographs of your wife in her wedding gown, and some of your two children. Those are away at school. You may not know this, Mr. Wilde, but head stewards are extremely well-paid people. Oh, and a wedding ring." She raised her head. "We did feel that, as this could be quite a dangerous assignment, we should go along with her, and allow her to take someone she knows well, and knows she can trust, and who she knows can trust her."

"Does she know all that?" Wilde asked.

"She says so. Will you take the job, Mr. Wilde?"

"When we have finished discussing the other aspects of the situation. Several thousand other aspects, if you are determined that I am going to be a mercenary."

"Oh dear," Jonquil said. "I forgot to mention it. There is only one thing Jonas considers more important than women and wine. And it isn't song."

Carmel Wane gave another frosty smile. "Six thousand a year, Mr. Wilde. In pounds sterling and tax free."

"Well," Jonquil began, and then changed her mind.

"Well, Mr. Wilde?" Carmel Wane asked.

"You haven't mentioned danger money."

"I should have thought that was included. This is a dangerous assignment, as I said."

"I wasn't talking about protecting the Prince. I was talking about having to accept Jonquil as my wife."

"You may beat her, if she nags," Carmel Wane said with great satisfaction. "And of course, in addition to whatever we put aside for you, you will be receiving your pay from the Prince himself. I should have thought that would be all right, even for you. Will you take the job?"

"Do I have any alternative?"

Carmel Wane was still smiling. "At the moment, probably not. But you will, of course, be good after you get out into the open air."

"Jonquil will see to that, will she?"

"I think so. But you want to remember that from the moment you step on board that yacht, or in fact, from the moment I leave this cabin, we are the only friends you have in the world, Mr. Wilde. If the Prince of Xanda were ever to find out that you are not what you pretend . . . well, as Jonquil has said, he is not yet *that* civilised." She got up again, held out her hand. "I'll say goodbye now. Congratulations on your marriage. I hope it will remain a happy one."

Her flesh was dry, and a moment later the hand was withdrawn. She climbed the ladder to the wheelhouse and disappeared.

"I think you need another cup of tea," Jonquil said.

ii

"It is a nice flat sea," Bunty pronounced. "It will take us about four hours to make Cabrera from here."

"Then there is no point in leaving now," Wilde said. "As we cannot arrive before dark. Whereas if we left at dawn, we'd be there for a late breakfast. Dawn is the best time to put to sea, don't you think? And I would like a last evening in civilised surroundings."

Jonquil began to shake her head.

"Oh, come now," Wilde said. "You're not really going to turn out to be a nagging wife, are you? That would be a terrible disappointment. Listen. Starting tomorrow, starting tonight, in fact, I promise to be absolutely good. I promise to do anything and everything you command. But you can't cut a man off in midstream, so to speak. I might die of deprivation. And anyway, haven't we got a wedding to celebrate?"

Jonquil gazed at Bunty, who shrugged.

"You guarantee not to touch a drop of anything hard, as from ten o'clock tonight?"

"Absolutely."

Still she hesitated. And then sighed. And then smiled. "Well . . . I'll tell you, I feel a little like celebrating myself. Have you thought that this could be a permanent assignment, Jonas? The Prince is obviously going to need protecting for years and years and years, at least until his oil wells run dry. Carmel said they are estimated to last for half a century."

"Come to think of it," Wilde said, "ten o'clock may have been an optimistic figure. Shall we go?" It was just after four, and time was getting short.

Bunty had returned with his clothes, and he was wearing a sports shirt over white pants, and flipflops. Jonquil was also wearing an open-necked shirt over white pants, and flipflops. The only difference was that her pants were somewhat tighter than his; he did not see how she could safely bend over. Supposing she wanted to.

Her shirt was also a tighter fit, but that figured; she was not wearing a bra.

She held his hand as they walked along the dock. "I really am *excited,* you know," she said. "To be near you at all, Jonas. You really do turn me on. And to be working with you, as well . . ."

"Carmel's orders?" he asked.

"What?" The eyes behind the glasses were wide and innocent.

"That you should snow me so hard and so continuously I won't have time to think."

"What a remark to make about your wife." She extended her left hand in front of her to look at the ring. "Shall we stop here?"

The two boys gazed at Wilde; the big one had his right hand in plaster.

"Not if you want to get back to the boat tonight," Wilde said.

She nodded thoughtfully, and allowed herself to be guided. The little streets were crowded, with hippies, with yachtsmen and their ladies, with genuine tourists, and with native Ibizans. Wilde escorted her through the crowd towards the central square, which was even more crowded.

"What we want is a nice little table on the road," he said.

"You'll be lucky," she grumbled. "Jonas. Why *don't* we go back to the ship, send Bunty for a walk instead. There's liquor on board."

"I like people," Wilde said. "Here we are." He sat her down, snapped his fingers. "Sangria, for two."

"*Sí señor,*" the boy said.

"Sangria doesn't do my figure any good," Jonquil said.

"So quit worrying; you're married now, remember?" He waited for the boy to come back. But she had to be occupied, somehow. He leaned across, took her hand. "I suppose I'm being a bit of a bore, or would boor be a better word? Quite a lot has happened today, wouldn't you say?"

"Quite a lot," she agreed. "But it has all turned out very well, wouldn't you say?"

"I'm reserving judgement on that."

"I suppose," she said thoughtfully, "that I had better practice calling you Rupert."

"Which is one of my reasons for reserving judgement. Tell me, how long have you had your eye on me?"

"For ten days," she said. "You really haven't been very sharp, recently."

"It hadn't occurred to me to be sharp, if you follow me. And so you contacted this Wane woman, and she told you to pick me up."

"That's right. I really am very happy she agreed."

"But it hadn't occurred to you to do it on your own? I mean, you're a good little girl who always takes orders?"

"I like to survive," she said.

"Oh, quite. What exactly is the relationship between you and Carmel? So she's the boss. But I have a feeling that her position is, what is the word I want? Equivocal?"

The boy brought the jug of sangria and two glasses, and Wilde poured.

"She is like me," Jonquil explained. "This particular branch of the Israeli Secret Service has recruited a large number of non-Jewish agents, for a number of understandable reasons. I happen to have been working for Tel Aviv for several years. I suppose I'm not very good, really. I'm still just a field operative. My business is observation. I'm decorative, I suppose, so I find it easy to obtain information. Carmel, now, belongs to a very special branch within the service. Really top secret hush hush sort of thing."

"And you're flattered that she has deigned to look at you at all."

"I like to feel I'm operating on a major level. Don't you?"

"I've never really operated on anything less," Wilde said. "Would you mind if I left you for a couple of minutes? I think my bladder is still full of tea."

Jonquil looked at her watch. "Two minutes, Jonas."

"Don't you trust me?" Wilde asked, and got up. He threaded his way through the tables and the doorway of the bar itself, found the boy who had served them. "Step over here," he suggested.

The boy obeyed.

"This is a thousand-peseta note," Wilde said. "And this is another one. That lady out there is my wife, whom I love dearly. Unfortunately, I have just seen another young woman who is not my wife, but whom I also love dearly. Savvy?"

"Oh yes, señor. But . . ."

"I wish to absent myself for fifteen minutes, without being noticed. So would you, next time you pass, absent-mindedly trip and empty as much liquid refreshment as you can over my wife?"

"But, señor . . ."

Wilde produced two more thousand-peseta notes. "You keep the lady occupied for fifteen minutes and you can have these as well. She's a practical soul; you'll have to souse her."

The boy grinned, and folded the first two notes into his palm. "I will do it, señor."

"I thought you might. Have fun."

Wilde rounded the bar, passed the scandalised gaze of the *patrón*, and found his way through the kitchen and out the back. He began to run; the Post Office was two blocks away and it was close to five. And he soon discovered that maybe Carmel Wane's estimate of his condition was more accurate than he would have admitted. Carmel Wane. Jonquil Malone. A man called Bunty. And a transparently absurd situation. They must suppose that he was totally blotto. Or they must have very little knowledge of the level of intelligence needed to survive twenty years as Her Majesty's Executioner.

Sweat poured down his face, and he staggered up the steps to the Post Office. It would be shut in ten minutes. But he had made it.

"I wish to send a telegram."

The girl pushed the form towards him.

"To *The Times* newspaper," Wilde explained as he wrote. "It is an advertisement for their Personal Column."

The girl took the form, scanned it.

"Would you read it back, please?" Wilde asked.

The girl shrugged, as if to indicate that if he was feeling funny, she had had a long day at that desk. *"In case of need,"* she read. *"Miss Majorca just and try Esmeralda."* She raised her head. "There is no such place."

"Who needs places?" Wilde said. "My friend is a crossword expert, and for relaxation he plays Scrabble."

Her eyebrows rose and fell, and she gave change. Wilde smiled at her, and began his return journey. He ran half the way and then slowed to a walk. He had to appear in breath and not too heavily sweated up. He regained the back door and felt his way through the bar to the table. His young friend was still mopping.

"Where is the señora?"

"Mamá took her upstairs, señor. For the sponge."

Wilde took out the two notes. "How long has she been gone?"

"Ten minutes, señor."

Wilde sat down. "And how long have I been sitting here?"

"Nine minutes, señor."

"When you take over the government," Wilde said. "Remember that it was my idea. Now bring another jug of sangria." He handed over the money, and a few moments later was pouring.

Just in time to greet Jonquil; her white pants were stained with purple blotches.

"Can't take you anywhere," Wilde said.

She was not amused. "Look at them," she said. "Ruined. I ought to break that child's neck."

"It all comes from leaving the top button undone," Wilde explained. "Any man looking down there gets cross-eyed. Any boy, now, would naturally lose his balance. Have another drink."

"I am going back to the ship," she said, speaking very slowly and distinctly. "And you are coming with me."

"Hen-pecked," Wilde grumbled. "I always knew it would be this way."

iii

Seen from the sea, Cabrera appears as the largest of a chain of rocks and islets which stretch southwards from Majorca, separated from the larger island by a five-mile-wide strait. The island itself appears also to be a solid and fairly substantial piece of rock. But once entry is made through the narrow channel at the north-western tip, under the vacant eyes of the old fort which dominates the narrows, it is discovered that in reality the impressive mountain is no more than a shell, and the entire centre of the island is a vast lagoon, some six fathoms deep at the edges and descending to considerably more than that in the middle, where an entire nineteenth-century fleet of war could be anchored in complete security. The half-dozen yachts which are all that are usually to be found here can therefore separate themselves to their heart's content, if they choose, and anchor well beyond earshot of their nearest neighbour.

And then their crews need do nothing, except swim, and bask on the deck. And occasionally take a drink. If they are allowed to. Wilde lay on the foredeck of the motor cruiser and felt the heat scorching his back, while a similar warmth rose from the heated teak to caress his chest and belly and thighs. Water still drained from his hair, and he thought that the sweetest thing in the world right this minute would be a very tall, very cold glass filled with rum and a few additives.

Instead he was vouchsafed a long look at Jonquil Malone's legs. They were delightful legs, a shade too thin and yet so splendidly muscled as to be sexy all in themselves. He had seen a lot of them these past few days. In bed and out of bed. She had been honeymooning, and there was no question but that she had been telling the truth when she had claimed that he turned her on. No one could act that well.

Well, she turned him on as well. She always had done, from the moment they had first met, so strangely on the bus out to the plane at Heathrow. Six years ago? And then he had still been suffering from the depression induced by Julie Ridout's death. Another woman, who had made the cardinal error of falling in love with Wilde, and who had died, suddenly and violently, and in Julie's case, he thought, painfully.

So Jonquil bothered him. Because she was getting too fond of him? Because there was no reason for it? Or because it could only end with her getting hurt? Even on an assignment as apparently innocuous as this?

Except that there was nothing at all innocuous about this assignment. Because there was nothing in the least innocuous about Carmel Wane, and therefore about the people for whom she worked.

And for whom Jonquil Malone also worked.

But all of those aspects of the situation had to be investigated, and he could not do that on his own. But they had been here for four days and there had been not the slightest ripple in reply to his cable. So maybe Mocka had stopped reading *The Times* after Wilde had walked out. Maybe the word was, drop Wilde. Maybe he *was* completely on his own.

What would he do then?

"Time for your exercises," Jonquil said.

"Give over," he said. "I've only been lying here for five minutes."

"You have been lying there for half an hour," she said, taking off her sombrero and tying a ribbon round her hair. "Come on, now. One hundred press-ups."

"Do you really imagine one hundred press-ups are going to do me the slightest bit of good, darling? My strength comes from my brain. So you had a point; when my brain is fuddled with drink I'm not so good. I haven't had a drop in four days. And I might as well make another point. You don't want to dry me out too much. Because like everything else the old wheels need an occasional oiling. I have existed on a couple of drinks a day, minimum, all my life. Right now . . ."

"You are an alcoholic," she said sweetly. "And in any event, Jonas dear, you are talking about getting your brain into the right shape to kill someone, remember? We don't want you to do that. Except in self-defence." She sat up to apply sun-tan lotion.

Wilde also sat up, to look at her. As the nearest company, except for Bunty, who apparently didn't matter, was a quarter of a mile away, she was taking the opportunity to do something about that all-over tan. And after all, he was on his honeymoon as well.

"Okay," he said. "So I'll do a hundred press-ups. But at least let me enjoy them."

She looked up, saw the expression on his face, and hastily scrambled to her feet. "Oh no," she said. "Oh no, no, no. Work and play do not mix."

She ran for the wheelhouse door.

Wilde got up more slowly. A large trawler yacht had entered the harbour perhaps an hour before, and anchored on the other side of the lagoon. Now its dinghy approached at speed, powered by an outboard motor. The sight brought Bunty from the wheelhouse, no doubt sent by Jonquil. Behind the wheel of the dinghy was a stout middle-aged gentleman with a bald head and a little moustache, wearing red and blue striped shorts.

"I say," he called. "Are you English?"

Bunty looked at Wilde, and Wilde grinned at the stout man. "What makes you think that?"

"Oh, just an idea, you know. In case of need, always look for an Englishman."

Wilde continued to grin. But the relief spreading upwards from his belly almost made him feel seasick. "And you'd be absolutely right, old man. By all means come alongside."

The outboard growled, and the dinghy came into the side of the boat.

"Terribly sorry to bother you, what," said the stout man. "But I wondered if either of you has any knowledge of engines."

"What sort of engines?" Wilde asked.

"Got trouble?" Bunty asked.

"Trouble," said the stout man. "I can't get the port thing to run at all."

"Flat battery," Bunty suggested.

"Oh no, really, the batteries are all right."

"What sort of engine?" Wilde asked again.

"Lehmann Fords. Do you know them?"

"I'm afraid not," Bunty said.

"I do," Wilde said. "I've always had Lehmann Fords in my boats."

"It'll be time for lunch in a moment," Jonquil said from the hatch. She had put on a black bikini which was bad for the blood pressure.

"I'll only be a moment," Wilde said. "I do think we should give Mr. . . . I never did catch your name, old man."

"Smith Horton," said Smith Horton. "I say, *do* you think you could look at them?"

"It'll be a pleasure," Wilde said, and grinned at Jonquil.

"Oh, bring your charming lady along too," Smith Horton said. "I'm sure my wife would like a bit of company."

"That's the first civilised offer I've had in days," Jonquil said, and lowered one long brown leg over the side.

Smith Horton waited for Wilde to settle himself, and then gunned the speedboat away from the side of the yacht. "Came down from Palma," he explained. "Just for the day, we thought. Only thirty miles, what? And then, just outside the entrance back there, the port engine suddenly cut right out. Just stopped, don't you know."

"Fuel blockage," Wilde suggested.

"It doesn't appear to be. I mean, I've done all the normal things, you know."

"Well, we'll have a look," Wilde said, and grinned at Jonquil. "Won't we?"

The dinghy was already coming under the side of the trawler, and a middle-aged woman, looking remarkably like the stout man, was waiting on deck. She handled a warp well.

"It's awfully good of you to come across like this," she said.

"Our pleasure." Jonquil climbed on board. "Must be very worrying having an engine go without warning. But my husband is quite good at that sort of thing."

"Why don't you show Mrs. . . . ?" The stout man smiled at Wilde. "I never got your name either, old man."

"Smart," Wilde said. "Rupert Smart. My wife's name is Jonquil."

"Well, as I was saying," Smith Horton said, clambering on board with some difficulty. "Why don't you show Jonquil the ship, Martha, and perhaps make us all an apéritif, while I show Rupert the engine."

"But I like engines too," Jonquil said.

"You won't like this one," Martha Smith Horton declared with great firmness. "Down there is a mass of oil and grease."

Smith Horton led the way forward, down the companion ladder to the fore cabin, and then through the bulkhead door leading aft to the engine room. There was not quite room to stand. "We need oil," he muttered. "I don't think she trusts us, old man."

"Sad, but true," Wilde agreed. "I think I had better lie in the stuff." He lay down, and Smith Horton hastily poured some oil on the deck for him to roll across. He thrust his head as far into the space beneath the engine block as he could manage. Smith Horton hovered just above him, handing him a hammer. "Must look as if you're trying."

"With a hammer?" Wilde asked. "She's more acid than dumb, you know."

"Mind you," Smith Horton said. "She's a good-looking young woman."

"And lots of fun," Wilde said. "She claims to work for the Israelis, and wants me to work for them too, in a rather hilarious position." Hastily he outlined his conversation with Carmel Wane.

"Carmel Wane," Smith Horton said thoughtfully. "We'll check her out, Wilde. Mind you, much of what she said was true. There have been several attempts on the life of the Prince of Xanda, and he has just bought himself a rather nice boat. I assume you would have no worries if the whole situation was genuine."

"I don't like the situation under any guise. I would also like to find out just how Jonquil knows so much about me. This bothered me years ago, but I never got around to checking it out. Anyway, we were somewhat closer to the Israelis than we are now."

"Yes," Smith Horton said. "You know, old man, if this is not genuine, there can be only one reason for them to attempt to employ you, of all people."

"Which would mean that something stinks in Tel Aviv."

"Yes. Except . . . I really don't see how they can force you to kill the old boy if you don't want to."

"Believe me," Wilde said. "I'm not sleeping very well, either. Which is why I want out."

"What exactly do you mean?"

"I propose to walk away from this outfit while I am still walking. If I have to damage anyone to do it, then I am prepared to damage anyone. I just wanted to put the lot of you in the picture regarding the situation around the Prince. I thought it might interest you."

"Oh, it does. Now there's something I have to ask you. I understand that you have failed to make contact for three months. I have no wish to become embroiled in departmental difficulties, old chap, but Commander Mocka asked me to discover just what you are at, if possible. Your intentions, and that sort of thing."

Wilde sighed. "Tell him to bail me out of this one and I'll buy him lunch."

"Ah. Then you are prepared to co-operate."

"Meaning?"

"That what you have told me is so very interesting that I simply must learn more. And there is no one at this moment quite so well placed as you. Just keep your nose clean, and be obstinate, and wait for me to be in touch again."

"Oh, great," Wilde said. "Do make it soon."

"Use the St. Tropez contact," Smith Horton said. "As you are going to be there soon enough." He raised his voice. "Then you think that must be it."

"Blocked jets," Wilde said firmly, and banged the engine once or twice with his hammer. "I'm afraid the best thing I can suggest is that you hobble back to Palma on one engine and have the whole lot cleaned out there."

"Um," Smith Horton said disconsolately. "Well, it was awfully good of you to look, old man. Now out you come and have a drink. The ladies have been working as well."

Wilde pushed himself backwards and stood up; the bulkhead door was open, and Martha Smith Horton and Jonquil Malone were crouching there, Jonquil balancing a tray of drinks on one knee.

"Rupert," she said disgustedly, "you look all slippery."

CHAPTER 4

Seen from the deck of a ship at the head of the gulf which bears its name, the village of St. Tropez looks just that. Only the large fortress which crowns the hill south of the port suggests an importance out of keeping with the huddled brown-roofed houses.

The illusion of a quiet, if perhaps historic, backwater does not last. The jetty makes the entrance to the harbour face roughly north, away from the open Mediterranean and towards the head of the gulf and the new yachting complex of Port Grimaud. The yacht therefore has to accomplish a U-turn to enter the harbour itself, and even in the case of a rather splendid boat like *Esmeralda* is immediately made to feel its proper size. For St. Tropez is always crowded, and invariably with at least a dozen of the millionaire variety of yacht, on which the crew outnumber the potential passengers, and the after deck is one continual cocktail party. Jonquil elected to dock *Esmeralda* at the other end of the harbour, on the new pontoons, where the berthing master obligingly found her a space. She handled the boat well, with Wilde forward to let go the anchor, and Bunty aft with the mooring lines. She did a lot of things well, he was realising. Not that he had ever doubted she would.

She also carried a grudge well. "We're due on board *Female Spirit* in half an hour," she said briefly. "So you can have a shower, Rupert, and then dress yourself properly."

Wilde nodded. They had come overnight from Cabrera, and it had taken them the better part of two days. They had been on auto pilot, but it had still required one of them to remain on watch the whole time. "Don't you think we should lie down for five minutes first?" he asked. "We want to appear bright and cheerful."

She regarded him as if he had been a spider. "I have more important things to do."

He grabbed her arm, pulled her gently but insistently down the stern companionway. "I told you, I never saw either of those people before in my life."

She kicked the door to the aft cabin shut behind her, perhaps without meaning to. "What do you propose to wear?"

"I have some proper yachting gear here; blue blazer, grey trousers, the lot. Will that do?"

"Very nicely." She opened the wardrobe and peered at her clothes. "I'll stick to my suit. You understand that the Prince is a bit of a lecher."

"Meaning I'm not supposed to get jealous?"

She lay across the bed. "It was marvellous at midnight. I'd have thought you might have joined me."

Wilde joined her. "I never did have that nap you promised me." He lowered his head. "Our first quarrel, after only a week of married bliss." He could hear her heart pounding just beneath his left ear; his eyes were blocked with soft flesh.

"No wife likes her husband to deceive her. What is more, if those people work for Mocka, you are being a double agent, and that is a serious business."

"You'd have to execute me," he suggested.

She sat up, and his head bounced down to her thighs. "You seem to think this whole thing is a joke. I suppose you feel, like so many English people, that the affairs of Israel and the Middle East are just a nuisance, and are even a nuisance only in so far as they might interfere with your precious oil supplies. Well, let me tell you, Jonas Wilde, there is more at stake right here in the Mediterranean than has been at stake around Britain for twenty years. Britain? My God, who'd be interested in that picked old bone."

"Rupert," he murmured.

"Eh?"

"You called me Jonas. You're supposed to be calling me Rupert."

"Oh, get knotted." His head did another bump, and she went to shower. But the water did not cool her off. "Are you going to spend the day lying there?" she demanded. "We have an appointment. And you had better be good."

"I shall be very good," he promised, and got dressed. "Tell me, what happens to Bunty and the ship?"

"A crew will be along," she said. "We're quite well organised, you know." She finished brushing her hair, arranged a large brimmed straw hat in place.

"Did anyone ever tell you that you are beautiful?" Wilde asked. "Seen from the back, of course."

She turned. "Jonas . . ."

"Rupert."

"Rupert. Don't you see, we can't work together if we don't trust each other?"

"How about my word."

She stared at him for some more seconds. "I might just settle for that. That those Smith Hortons or whatever they were called were absolutely genuine?"

Wilde sighed. "I don't know. They may well have been on a dirty week-end and not married at all. But those jets were blocked, darling. I give you my word. I have never seen either of them before, and I really will be surprised if I ever see either of them again."

"And that will have to do. Say bye-bye to Bunty. If all goes well, you *will* be seeing him again. When you come back to collect our gear." She went ashore, and Wilde followed. They found their way through the crowds which always seem to throng the St. Tropez waterfront, French townspeople out for the day, French fishermen in dirty smocks and well-used sea boots, genuine tourists in outlandish but crisp and clean clothes, yachtsmen in shorts or blazers, and their women varying equally from bikinis to long skirts and dangling earrings, and hippies, wearing whatever garments they could put together and apparently wearing them for about the seventeenth consecutive day. The still air boiled with chatter, in a dozen languages, wares were hawked, anything from shell-fish to cheap ornaments to straw hats, waiters leaned in the doorways of the cafes, mentally separating the possible customers from those who obviously could not afford the tariffs, while the occasional pair of gendarmes strolled by, superciliously ignoring everyone.

And everyone stopped to look at the yachts. For they were now in the main part of the town, and the row of sterns facing them did not come to much under five million pounds, Wilde estimated very roughly. Which said nothing for the people on board. As it was still early morning, those visible consisted mainly of crew. But the gangplanks were down, decorated with deep-pile carpet, bearing the round symbol, rather like a road sign, which forbade entry to anyone wearing hard shoes or high heels, and to reinforce the sign, at the ship's end of each gangplank there waited a large sailor, arms folded, gazing at the passers-by with undisguised hostility.

The fourth yacht they came to bore the name *Female Spirit* on her stern, and her flag was Panamanian.

"So here we go," Wilde whispered. "Hold tight."

He approached the *passerelle,* and the large brown-skinned seaman slowly shook his head from side to side.

"We have an appointment. With Señor Albarana? The capitano? My name is Smart, and this is my señora."

The man stared at them some more, and then snapped his fingers. From the doorway to the saloon behind him there appeared an extremely good-looking girl, tall and slender and fine-boned, light-skinned but with long black hair framing thin, sensitive features and deep black eyes; she wore a short black dress beneath a white apron.

"We have applied for the job," Wilde said. "I am a steward, and my wife is very good. At the housekeeping."

"You come behind me," the girl said.

"Any time," Wilde agreed, and smiled at Jonquil. "After you, my dear."

Her face was expressionless, but there was a lot going on behind her eyes. She climbed the gangplank and tripped over a hatch cover situated just inside the rail; Wilde grabbed her arm.

"It is very early," the girl said. "You are the first."

"We need the job," Wilde said.

She smiled at him, quickly and shyly, and led them through the saloon. At least, presumably, it would be described as a saloon, Wilde thought. It was a large enclosed area surrounding a sunken swimming pool. There were no chairs but a variety of divans along each outer bulkhead, and the carpet was Persian. Forward there were double doors to a proper saloon, a place of soft leather armchairs, a desk, and an enormous television set. Forward of this again there was a small lobby, to the left of which was a fully equipped bar, as Carmel Wane had prophesied, while to the right there was a circular staircase. In front of them, Wilde was relieved to see, there was actually a bridge deck, with more instrumentation than Concorde. And they were on the right ship; he knew bullet-proof glass when he saw it.

"The wall," said the girl. "Will you face the wall, please, and put your hands on it?"

"Eh?"

"I think she means to search us, darling," Jonquil said. "My God."

For the girl did mean to search them, and had already started on Jonquil. It was quite the most thorough business Wilde had ever seen, as from a small cupboard let into the bulkhead she took what might have been a miniature vacuum cleaner and expertly passed it over every inch of Jonquil's body. A pad hung beside the plug for the metal detector, and on this she made notes from time to time, in a language Wilde did not understand. When she was finished with the detector, she made one or two additional investigations with her fingers, before turning to Wilde.

"Studied anatomy, have you?" he asked.

She gave him a quick smile, but did not slacken her efforts until she was satisfied that he was unarmed. Or was she? She prodded him in the small of the back.

"A safety pin," he explained. "Just a safety pin. It holds the lining into my blazer. I told you, we need the job."

The girl nodded.

"I think we have each been criminally assaulted," Jonquil remarked, trying to get her skirt straight. "I'm glad I was here to protect you. Is this your only job, searching people?" she asked.

But the girl was descending the staircase; this ended in another lobby, from which another pair of double doors led aft to a magnificent dining saloon, panelled in walnut and containing a walnut dining table which, Wilde calculated, would seat twelve at a pinch, although there were only six chairs present. Here the door forward led to another saloon, which, from the strictly utilitarian furnishing, belonged to the crew. And here a short, stout man with greying black hair and a dark complexion was seated at a desk, writing. He wore a blue jacket with gold braid on the shoulders and cuffs.

"Mr. and Mrs. Smart," the girl said. "They have come about the position."

Captain Albarana picked up one of the cards in front of him. "Ah." He looked at Wilde first, and then at Jonquil. It took him longer to look at Jonquil. Then he stood up and held out his hand. "Good day, Mrs. Smart. Good day, Mr. Smart. It is good of you to be punctual."

Jonquil watched her fingers being kissed, and smiled for the first time since leaving Cabrera. "It is our pleasure to be here, Captain."

"Sit down, please, and you, Mr. Smart. That will be all, Halma."

The girl nodded, and left.

"Does she play, too?" Wilde asked.

Captain Albarana raised his eyebrows.

"My husband occasionally supposes he is being funny," Jonquil said.

"Ah. The sense of humour," the captain said sadly. "It is good. Mr. Watt has a great sense of humour. Now, Mr. Smart, you understand that the duties we require will be that of a general steward. You will supervise the serving of meals, the making of drinks, and all the domestic arrangements of the ship."

"You mean I have a staff?" Wilde asked.

"But of course. There is the chef, and then there is the girl Halma, whom you have just met . . ."

"How very nice," Wilde murmured.

"And your wife, of course."

"What fun."

"Mrs. Smart will be in charge of the cabins aft. There are three cabins, along there." He pointed through the dining room. "And a fourth room below. You may use Halma to assist you there as well."

"Oh, I shall," Jonquil said. "Believe me."

"General dogsbody, Halma, is she?" Wilde asked.

Captain Albarana smiled at him. "She is a very obliging girl. A hard worker. I am sure you will get on well. If, of course, you and Mrs. Smart get the job. There will be other applicants along today, you understand."

"Oh, we do," Wilde said. "I have some testimonials with me. Claridge's, you know. We enjoyed Claridge's. And they were very sorry to see us go. And then there is one here from the Waldorf-Astoria, and one from the Trinidad Hilton, and . . ."

"I am sure they are all in order." Captain Albarana placed them on his desk without looking at them. "But of course Mr. Watt demands certain special qualities from his employees, which are far more important than mere references." He continued to smile.

"I'm sure," Wilde said. "Perhaps we could be told what these qualities are?"

The captain had stopped smiling, and was rising to his feet. "I think Mr. Watt will prefer to tell you himself, Mr. Smart. You will please rise." He bowed. "I wish you to meet your prospective employer, Mr. Watt."

ii

"You bow," whispered the captain, and Wilde and Jonquil each obeyed, Jonquil managing to turn hers into a curtsey, which combined operation was only feasible for a contortionist.

"You may rise," the Prince of Xanda said, his voice very soft, with the peculiarly liquid quality of the Arab.

Wilde straightened. He was impressed. The Prince was a tall man, but surprisingly slight. His face was thin, like his body, with a large nose, only faintly hooked, and a prominent chin. He was bareheaded, and his hair was black speckled with grey, but his beard was pure black, short and neatly clipped. His eyes were also black, and enveloping. His gaze swept over Wilde, and moved on to encompass Jonquil even more completely.

"What an attractive couple," he remarked to the woman by his side.

Who was worth a long stare all to herself. She was remarkably small, not a great deal more than five feet tall, Wilde estimated, a mere wisp of a figure, but one which, as displayed in a red bikini, suggested merely that he was looking through the wrong end of a telescope; breasts might be minute, waist infinitesimal, legs hardly more than matchsticks, but every inch of her body was magnificently proportioned, and even more magnificently shrouded in absolutely straight brown hair which reached past her thighs. Her features were no less perfectly fitted into the whole, small and delicate and alive, from the pointed chin, past the suddenly wide mouth and the flaring nostrils, to the green eyes, which darted at Wilde and left him feeling as naked as beneath the hands of the girl Halma. If she was a sample of what he was going to encounter on this voyage, it was just as well he was on his honeymoon.

"Indeed, Mr. Watt," she murmured, her voice hardly more than a whisper, her eyes still impaling Wilde.

But there was another person in the room, a large, moon-faced young man, young, as obviously Xandan as the Prince himself, also wearing a lounge suit, also gazing at Wilde. His face was expression-less, and it was difficult even to decide if there was any intelligence in his eyes. But the stare was unblinking.

"They are the first applicants for the positions of steward and housekeeper, Mr. Watt," Captain Albarana said. "Mr. and Mrs. Smart."

"Ah," Prince Walid agreed. "Have you employed them?"

"Well, sir, there are other applicants coming along later this morn-ing. I was going to have Mr. Smart give a demonstration of his art as a maker of cocktails."

The woman whispered something, standing next to the Prince. He inclined his head, listened, and smiled. His eyes were directed towards Jonquil.

"Yes," he said. "Madeleine councils well, Captain. By all means have Mr. Smart shake us a cocktail. Tell me, Mr. Smart, what can you do?"

Wilde uttered a silent prayer. "You have but to name your wish, sir."

"It is a habit I have but recently taken up, you understand," said Mr. Watt. "So I am still experimenting." His English was perfect, with only a trace of his Boston education remaining. "This morning, as it is still early, I would like a Blue Moon."

"A Blue Moon," Jonquil said. "One of Rupert's favourites. Isn't it one of your favourites, Rupert?" She was definitely nervous.

"Of course, sir," Wilde said. "Providing the necessary ingredients are on board."

"Everything you can possibly wish is on board, Smart," said Cap-tain Albarana.

"Including Crème de Yvette?"

"Of course." Mr. Watt smiled. "But you have already proved your point. Nevertheless, Smart, make the drink, for six, and we will cele-brate your appointment."

Wilde bowed. "Immediately, sir." He went up the stairs.

"But what about the other applicants, sir?" Albarana asked.

"When they come, tell them that the position is already filled. Un-less, of course, Smart manages to poison us." His smile spread into a grin, and the grin into a gust of loud laughter, in which the woman Madeleine and the captain dutifully joined. Jonquil managed to raise a nervous titter. The large young man's expression never changed.

Wilde was already mixing an ounce and a half of Crème de Yvette with three ounces of dry gin and an ounce and a half of lemon juice into the jug where he had placed the cracked ice. He found chilled cocktail glasses in the huge fridge, and a moment later, after a vigorous stir, he poured the six drinks. "Six Blue Moon cocktails, sir."

Mr. Watt smiled at him. "The first is for you, Smart. Will you try it, please?"

"Me, sir?"

"I said we would celebrate your position, Smart. But I must confess that I am a bit of a hypochondriac, and my great fear is of having my stomach upset. It can so easily happen, can it not? So your duties as steward will include tasting my food, and my drink, before I do. You have no objection?"

Wilde gazed at Jonquil, and Jonquil gazed at Wilde, her eyebrows apparently trying to apologise. Then he picked up the nearest glass and raised it. "To your health, Mr. Watt. And mine." He sipped, and nodded in appreciation.

"Thank you, Mr. Smart," Mr. Watt said. "I will take that one. You may have the second. Ladies. Captain?" He drank, and beamed at them. "You will do well on board *Female Spirit,* Smart. And Mrs. Smart, of course. You have the position."

"How very kind of you, sir," Wilde said. "I shall just step ashore and get our bags, shall I?"

"I'll come with you," Jonquil said.

"I'm sure that won't be necessary," Mr. Watt said. "Come with me, and I shall show you the staterooms, and your other duties." He glanced at Wilde. "Do hurry, Smart. Now this all-important position has been filled, we shall leave in half an hour."

"Indeed, sir? Can you tell me where we shall be going?"

The Prince of Xanda continued to smile. "Who knows? I will not know myself, until I think of a place."

iii

Wilde hurried. He had never felt quite so upset in his life, and he had made the cocktails. Bunty was on the dock, sitting on top of two suitcases.

"What has happened to *Esmeralda?*" Wilde demanded.

"Her relief crew arrived five minutes after you left," Bunty explained. "She's gone to her next assignment."

"And you're stuck with an economy fare," Wilde said. "Would you mind letting me have our bags?" They had been carefully prepared by Jonquil, looked sufficiently battered, and had various travel tags pasted from end to end.

"You've got the job, then," Bunty decided, getting up.

"As you say. I presume you are going to be in touch with Miss Wane?"

"I imagine she'll be getting in touch with me, to make sure you got on board."

"Well, you can tell her from me that I expect my pay to be doubled. He's employing me less as a steward than as his taster."

Bunty raised his eyebrows. It was too reminiscent of Jonquil for comfort. "Tricky. But not as dangerous as you might think, you know. As it is well known that the Prince of Xanda has all his food and drink tasted, who would dream of wasting time in trying to poison him?"

"What a splendid fellow you are," Wilde said. "If there weren't so many ignorant optimists in the world I might almost feel healthy again. Don't forget my message for Carmel."

He lifted a suitcase in each hand, hurried away, drifted down a side street leading away from the harbour, and found the right junk shop. He discovered he was out of breath, and it occurred to him that for the first time in a long while he was actually a little frightened. He was used to death coming towards him in a variety of forms, but all of them visible. And he did not even know the chef on board the yacht. Yet.

"Can I help you, monsieur?" The woman was middle-aged, dark, and petite.

"I thought perhaps a cigarette lighter," Wilde said. "Mine is broken, and I always say, in case of need there is nothing quite like a good cigarette lighter."

"Ah," said the woman. "I am afraid we have nothing like that in stock. There has not been sufficient time for our goods to come in, you understand. You are staying in St. Tropez?"

"Unfortunately, no. I am leaving in half an hour."

"Ah," she said again. "Then you can give me a forwarding address? Or perhaps, if you will tell me where you are going, I could direct you to a shop which might have the thing you want."

"There's the problem," Wilde said. "I have no idea where I am going, at this moment."

"Oh dear," the woman said. "That is unfortunate." She smiled brightly. "I think the best thing you can do is keep away from fire in any form, as you have not got the proper materials at hand. And perhaps get in touch when you return to St. Tropez."

Wilde looked over his shoulder. The shop was for the moment empty. "*I* think the best thing I can do is jump ship, madame. I don't like my situation."

The woman's smile faded, and he realised that she had very hard eyes. "That would not be good, monsieur," she said. "Not only would you be abandoning your charming wife to a terrible fate, but you would be letting down the side. I do not think we would like that. I think we would have to regard you as having changed teams."

Wilde gazed at her. So she was no mere messenger girl. Well, he had not really supposed she was. "I'll have red roses, top and bottom of the coffin," he said, and returned to the waterfront, feeling only slightly more unhappy. But why should they hurry to the assistance of a man who had walked away in a huff. He was surprised that they had taken any notice of his telegram at all. And now he must prove himself a good boy by staying put. So maybe things weren't as bad as he feared they might be.

The huge yacht was being prepared for sea. There were five sailors on deck, in blue canvas trousers and blue sweaters. If Carmel Wane was right, and they were all picked members of the Xandan secret police, presumably they were safe enough. And the captain was on the bridge, checking his various pressure gauges. Spanish. But obviously an old acquaintance of the Prince. Although that didn't necessarily mean a thing.

Well, then, the women? Or was he worrying unnecessarily? There was no hesitation in letting him on board this time. But Halma was waiting in the otherwise deserted lounge, giving that serious smile.

"I know, I know, sweetheart," Wilde agreed. He laid the suitcases on the deck at the top of the spiral staircase, and flipped them open. She ran the metal detector over the top layer of clothes, turned them back to check Wilde's shaver and various bits and pieces in Jonquil's bag, and seemed satisfied.

"Thank you, Mr. Smart."

"We are obviously going to know each other so well, within such a short space of time," Wilde pointed out, "that I think you should call me Rupert."

She smiled, and returned to the saloon. Wilde went down the staircase to the galley deck, poked his nose into the very spacious kitchen, discovered a busy little man with long moustaches, actually wearing a chef's hat.

"Good morning," he said. "I am Ruper Smart."

"Ah, Mr. Smart," said the chef. "Good morning to you. I am Bruno della Guardia."

His voice contained no trace of any accent whatever. He would have to be fished.

"Don't tell me," Wilde said. "Naples, via the Bronx and Soho."

"Ah, Mr. Smart, no. Sorrento, via Miami Beach and Bournemouth. It is much better." Bruno della Guardia held out his hand. "Welcome, welcome. We work together, yes?"

"Very much yes. You know I'm lumbered with tasting Mr. Watt's food?"

"Ah, no?" Bruno looked properly shocked. "*My* food?"

"Ah, yes," Wilde said. "So keep it light, will you, old man? I have a nervous stomach."

Bruno grinned at him. "Ah, Mr. Smart, we work together, you and me."

"That, I like the sound of. Rupert is the name." He listened to the sound of the huge General Motors diesels starting to growl beneath his feet. "I'd better dump this gear. Any idea where I sleep?"

"I will show you to your cabin, Mr. Smart," Halma said from his shoulder. Now, how long had she been there, he wondered?

He followed her down the continuation of the spiral staircase, arrived at a deck on a level with the engine room, he figured; the huge hum came from beyond a bulkhead immediately aft of the staircase. Halma went forward, down a narrow corridor, opened a door into a comfortable double cabin; the bunks were an upper and a lower. There was also a dressing table with a mirror, and she opened an inner door to show him the bathroom. "This you share," she said.

"With you?"

"And with Captain Albarana," she explained. "The crew have their own, forward."

"Sounds entrancing." Wilde put down the suitcases. "Have you any idea where my wife is?"

"She is aft, looking at the staterooms." Halma gazed at him.

"Ah, yes," Wilde said, taking his cue from Bruno. "Tell me something, Halma. Who tasted the owner's food before I came along?"

"I did, Mr. Smart."

"And you're looking fit enough, I'm glad to see. And now you're my sidekick, is that right?"

She frowned her bewilderment.

"I mean, you're here to help me, right? To assist me?"

She nodded. "You have but to command me, Mr. Smart."

"That is going to be a great pleasure. But in these circumstances, my first command just has to be that you call me Rupert. Now tell me, you have been with Mr. Watt a long time?"

"Mr. Watt has been very kind to me, Mr. Smart."

"Rupert."

"Rupert."

"That's my girl. Now, it is essential for me to know who is on board, if I am going to be a good steward, right? Come, sit down." He patted the bunk beside him, and she sat there, continuing to gaze at him with those wide dark eyes. "There are five crew members?"

She nodded.

"And they have all been with Mr. Watt a long time too?"

"Oh yes."

"And Captain Albarana?"

"This is a new ship," Halma explained. "Captain Albarana knew Mr. Watt before, I think. But this is the first time they have sailed together."

"Ah, yes. And then there are Bruno and yourself. Bruno an old employee like everyone else?"

"Oh no. He came yesterday."

"Ah, bother," Wilde said. His stomach was beginning to feel queasy again. "Were there no other applicants?"

"Oh yes, Rupert. But Bruno was easily the best."

"Of course. Then there are my wife and I. Now, what about the owner's party. Who is this woman, Madeleine?"

"She is Mr. Watt's friend," Halma said. "Mr. Watt always has a friend with him. Sometimes more than one."

"But at present there is only Madeleine?"

"At present. I believe we are going to pick up some more people shortly."

"I see. And the large young man? Do you know, he wasn't introduced."

"He is Splendide."

"No doubt he is, at certain things."

"That is his name. Splendide. He is Mr. Watt's bodyguard."

"But not his taster? There is going to have to be a union meeting about this. Well, you have been very helpful, Halma. If I think of anything else I want I'll let you know."

"My cabin is across the corridor," she said. "It is a double, but there is only me at present." Her gaze was unchanging.

"Now, that is probably the most valuable piece of information you have given me yet," he agreed. "Oops."

Because the door was opening, to reveal Jonquil. A Jonquil with pink spots in her cheeks and some difficulty breathing. "Am I interrupting something?"

"Halma was just leaving," Wilde explained.

Halma left.

"I wondered if you'd got back," Jonquil said. "Seeing as how we've cast off. Do you think it would be breaking the rules for the housekeeper to have a drink?"

"You may be my guest," Wilde said. "Had a hard time?"

"Christ Almighty," she remarked. "He showed me the cabins himself."

"Oh yes?"

"He told me that women are his hobby."

"Lucky fellow."

"That he just liked to look at them and touch them, and see how they worked."

"And did you? Work, I mean."

"He said he wanted to examine me."

"To see how you worked?"

"And he did. I think he must have trained as a doctor."

"And what was the upshot of all that?" Wilde asked.

"I know I'm not pregnant."

"You amaze me," Wilde said. "Presumably he will wish to carry his investigations a stage further, whenever he has the time."

"I'm not sure I could go along with that."

"You damned well will," Wilde said. "If I am going to be forced to taste every sheep's testicle that is served up to his nibs, you can at least humour the human variety. Meanwhile, if there is a rotten apple on board, it is my estimate that it must consist of either the captain, the chef, or the young woman named Madeleine. So keep your eye on those three."

"And not Halma?" Her tone was frosty.

"Halma does not quite fit the bill. If I were you, I'd change into something a little more ship-like, and join me upstairs." He closed the door behind him, climbed the spiral staircase. *Female Spirit* was already clear of the Gulf of St. Tropez, and steaming south-east at fourteen knots, he estimated. The land was falling rapidly astern, the mountains were becoming the northern horizon. Corsica? Or even farther?

But thought was complicated by duty. There was already a customer in his bar. The woman, Madeleine, wearing the bottom half of her bikini.

iv

"I was just becoming desperate," she remarked. "I will have . . ." She gazed at him, her lips just suggesting a smile. "A Blue Monday."

Wilde found it difficult to concentrate; there was a cool breeze filtering through the saloons.

"You do know how to make a Blue Monday?" she asked.

"Is this another test?" He cracked ice into the cocktail shaker, measured an ounce and a half of vodka.

"Of course. I'd like you to join me."

"My dear young woman," Wilde said. "If I am going to have to have a cocktail every time I make one, you are going to get some very odd drinks by lunchtime. I'll taste it for you, I promise." He poured in the half ounce of Cointreau, rattled the shaker.

"You do that almost professionally," she observed. "Have you a spare block of ice?"

Wilde took one from the fridge. "Don't you think I ought to rattle a shaker professionally?"

She slid the ice gently over her nipples. Clearly she was expecting the Prince and wanted to look her best. "I don't think you are a professional barman, if that is what you are trying to establish. Why did you apply for this job, Mr. Smart?"

"Did you spot the salary advertised?" He poured the drink. "Not even Claridge's could quite measure up." He tasted. "Not bad, if you like this sort of thing."

She drank, watching him over the rim of the glass; the ice cube was returned to the bar, its mission accomplished. "I think you are a fraud, Mr. Smart."

He removed the cube and wiped the marble clean. "Isn't the drink all right?"

"The drink is delicious. You are delicious. Just too delicious. Did anyone tell you what my function is on board this ship?"

Wilde polished glasses. It took his mind off the problems growing in front of him. "I hate to be indelicate, but I had assumed that was obvious to all."

"I am Mr. Watt's personal bodyguard," she said.

"I was told Splendide did that."

"Splendide is my back-up man. But of course my duty involves watching over Mr. Watt day and night, when Splendide could be only an embarrassment. I am not allowed to do very much relaxing."

"He seems a very apprehensive person, our employer," Wilde remarked. "Another?"

"I'll wait for Mr. Watt," she said. "You have no idea why he should be so careful?"

"I would say he must be a very wealthy man," Wilde said. "So perhaps he made some enemies while he was accumulating."

She gazed at him for some seconds, thoughtfully, and then smiled at the doorway. "I was testing some more of Smart's quite exceptional abilities."

The Prince of Xanda wore a pair of crimson bathing trunks. Wilde found it even more difficult to calculate his age. He looked very fit, and the thinness was mainly some rather useful-looking muscles.

"Blue Mondays, sir," he said. "Can I make another?"

"Vodka, no," said the Prince. "What about an El Presidente?"

Wilde did some more rapid remembering.

"You *can* make an El Presidente, Smart?" Madeleine inquired.

"I can try, miss," Wilde said, taking out the bottle of white rum, the French vermouth, the curaçao, and the grenadine.

"I think you like your work, Smart," the Prince remarked. "I will have it in the pool."

He walked across the inner lounge and plunged into the water.

"Seems odd to have a pool indoors," Wilde said. "Why cruise the Med and shut yourself away behind glass? Might as well be in the North Sea."

The woman smiled coldly. "Mr. Watt likes to keep the world at arm's length." She watched him rattle the second shaker. "Been married long?"

"Six years." Wilde poured, placed the glass on a silver tray, came round the bar, and made his way aft. *Female Spirit* had set up a long, slow roll which was fairly easy to anticipate.

The Prince stood at the shallow end, up to his chest in water, took the glass and held it up. Wilde tasted it. "Very good, sir, if I say so myself."

The Prince drank. "Good," he said. "I have invited Mrs. Smart to join me for a dip. Do you object?"

"Of course not, sir."

"Good. Well, mix up another batch of those, will you. Make one for yourself as well, and then tell Madeleine to entertain you."

Wilde nodded. There was certainly no coyness about this fellow. He returned to the bar, just in time to watch Jonquil coming through the doorway; she wore her black bikini.

"Oh, very nice," Madeleine remarked. "I think Mr. Watt will like that. Although he may think there is rather too much of it."

Jonquil passed without looking at either of them, cramming her hair into a bathing cap. There were pink spots back in her cheeks.

Wilde mixed the cocktails. "Mr. Watt suggested I let you entertain me. I must say, he seems to be very democratic. For a millionaire."

Madeleine gazed at him.

"Or have I said the wrong thing?"

"I don't know," she said. "But I will entertain you, Mr. Smart. Come with me."

"The owner said . . ."

"The owner will not miss us for a while, Smart." She slipped off the bar stool and went to the stairs, glanced over her shoulder. "Really."

She went down the stairs, and encountered the girl Halma. "Come with me," she said again.

Halma nodded, glanced at Wilde, and waited for him to pass her. Wilde followed Madeleine, terribly aware of the girl walking silently behind him. Vague alarm bells were sounding off in his brain, but he didn't know what they were trying to say.

Madeleine reached the crew's quarters, and now she opened the door of Wilde's cabin.

"How very cosy," he said. "Does Halma come in too?"

"I think she may be useful," Madeleine said. "Close the door, Halma."

"Which is even cosier," Wilde said. "I think I should warn you that I am no longer in my first youth."

"Would you place your suitcases on the lower bunk, please," Madeleine said, suddenly very efficient. "And open them?"

"I assume that you have a warrant? Oh, don't get all riled up. Just my little joke. Halma has already done this bit."

"That is correct, Madeleine," Halma said. "I searched the suitcases when they came on board."

"Then Mr. Smart has nothing to worry about, has he?" Madeleine said. "I will just check."

Wilde shrugged, placed the two suitcases side by side on the bunk, flipped the lids.

"Thank you," Madeleine said. "You may stand there and watch me, of course. I have no desire to be accused of having stolen anything."

"Don't give it a thought," Wilde said, and watched her flicking through his spare shirts and underclothes, running her hands into the side pockets.

"There is nothing there," Halma said.

"My God." Madeleine straightened, holding something in her hand.

"Found my French letters?" Wilde inquired. "I don't know why I carry them, nowadays, as you girls are all so well protected. I suppose it's for auld lang syne, don't you know."

"Quick, Halma," Madeleine shouted, closing the suitcase and backing against the bunk.

Wilde turned to face the younger woman, found himself gazing down the barrel of a small automatic pistol.

CHAPTER 5

"This is rather sudden," Wilde said. "Do you always carry one of those in your pocket?"

The girl's face remained expressionless, but her eyes were hard.

"He's dangerous, Halma," Madeleine whispered. "You don't know how dangerous. If he makes the slightest move, shoot him down."

She began to sidle towards the door. Halma remained still, moving slightly in time to the roll of the ship, the gun muzzle still pointing at Wilde's belly; there was a faint paleness on her knuckle where it wrapped around the trigger, and it occurred to Wilde that he was in a somewhat dangerous position, even before Madeleine got outside.

"Am I allowed to ask why you are behaving in this ridiculous fashion?" he asked. "Or is this some form of initiation ceremony?"

Madeleine had reached the door. "We shall see," she said, "what Mr. Watt makes of this." She waved the object she had apparently taken from his suitcase, which appeared to be something rather like a driving licence.

Wilde frowned. "Would it help if I told you that I had never seen that before in my life?"

"Look out," Madeleine screamed, at the same time leaping for the door and dragging on the handle.

Halma's head jerked, and her eyes came to life. Wilde realised that he was about to die, and that this was Madeleine's intention, and no doubt had been her intention since she had entered the cabin. But long before the thought crystallised in his brain he was already moving, hurling himself to one side, listening to the explosion of the pistol, hearing the whumpff as the bullet sliced into the bed-clothes behind where he had been standing.

As he fell, he kicked, swinging the toes of his yachting shoes into the girl's shin. She gave an unladylike grunt and fell forward, but she was turning as she did so, and she still held the gun. Wilde had to propel himself from the floor the moment he touched it, using his hands as spring-boards to thrust himself upwards and away, moving to one side and reaching for the girl all in the same instant.

She rolled on her back, her short skirt and her apron flying, and he looked at nothing but leg. More muscular than he had supposed, and ending in feet meant for his belly. Nor could he now stop himself. He took the flailing toes in the solar plexus, gasped for breath, but closed his hands on her ankles as he did so, exerting all his strength as he fell backwards so that she was in turn jerked from the deck and into the air. She fired a third time as she left the floor, but there was no time to aim; the bullet shattered the mirror on the dressing table. Then she fell on top of Wilde. On the way down she met his fist coming up; there was no time to think of any other way of coping with a situation which had suddenly gone mad. The closed fingers took her on the chin, and she collapsed in an unconscious heap in the middle of Wilde's blazer. And still her fingers clutched the gun.

Wilde rolled off her and scrambled to his feet. The cabin door swung wide; Madeleine had disappeared, but in her place there was a sailor, large and brown skinned, unarmed but no doubt sufficiently well trained, as Jonquil had intimated.

And there was another problem.

But only when he could spare the time. The sailor was starting to come in, and Wilde was in a hurry to get out. As the Xandan policeman reached for him, apparently thinking in terms of a bear hug, Wilde seized the extended wrists, ducked, and swung his thigh into the man's groin. The sailor gave a howl of alarm and shot over Wilde's back, fortunately missing Halma and landing on the side of the bunk, from whence he fell to the floor.

Wilde reached the corridor, slammed the door behind him. He could hear nothing above the steady throb of the engines. But Madeleine would have gone up, he reckoned. He seized the hand-rail and dragged himself up the spiral staircase, four at a time. On the next level Bruno della Guardia ran out of the galley; the two men collided, and landed together on their hands and knees.

"For God's sake," Wilde protested.

"There is much noise," Bruno explained. "Are we going to sink?"

"Very likely," Wilde gasped. "Stay at your post, old chum."

There was shouting from above him. He scrambled up the remaining steps, reached the bar, and found another large sailor waiting for him. This one carried a short length of thick rubber hose, no doubt standard equipment for the Xandan secret police. He stepped forward as Wilde reached the top of the stairs, and the powerful rubber flicked from side to side. But Wilde was underneath it, ducking and straightening, hands brought together and clasped to sideswipe into the man's belly; air exploded, and the sailor fell forward, to have his chin encounter the same pair of hands swinging back up again, crunching into his jaw, knocking him unconscious long before he reached the deck.

Wilde leapt over him, ran through the lounge, and stopped at the entrance to the swimming pool. Here he was faced by the woman Madeleine, panting, by Captain Albarana, and by the Prince of Xanda. The Prince held Jonquil Malone, by the arms from behind; they still stood in the pool, waist deep in water, and no doubt at his insistence she had removed her bra. She stared at Wilde with an expression of utter horror.

"Call the crew," Madeleine commanded, her voice shrill. "Call the crew, Captain. Quickly."

Albarana started to make for the door to the deck.

"I do not think that will be necessary, Captain," the Prince said. "I am sure this gentleman, whoever he is, has a great deal of common sense, and will be prepared to understand the situation in which he now finds himself. Especially as we hold his wife, do we not?"

His fingers had moved up to Jonquil's neck. She gave a faint shrug of the shoulders, as if she would have tugged free, but the Prince was stronger than he appeared, and garrotting people was his hobby.

Wilde had to agree that he had a point.

ii

And then he realised that the point wasn't valid at all, that if someone should choose to wring Jonquil Malone's neck right this minute he would be saved a lot of trouble.

It occurred to him that he had never been so angry in his life.

But the moment's delay had been fatal. Now there were men behind as well as in front of him. "I don't suppose it would help if I said I have no idea what this is all about?" he asked.

The Prince of Xanda released Jonquil reluctantly. "You must not take us for fools, Mr. Smart."

"Wilde," Madeleine said, consulting the little booklet she had taken from the suitcase. "It is all here, in his identity card. His name is Jonas Wilde. I am truly sorry, Excellency. I deserve to be punished." The Prince of Xanda smiled. "If you thought he might be genuine, my dear, then at least it was you who also had the first suspicion. You won't tell me what aroused your doubt." He climbed from the pool. "Wilde," he said. "And of course you know who I am, really. And thus were sent here to assassinate me, Mr. Wilde."

"Does what your girl friend claims to have found tell you that?" Wilde asked. "Oh, I know who you are, Excellency, but do stop to think a moment. If I really was a hired assassin, would I wander around with positive identification in my luggage? This thing is so transparently absurd it is almost funny."

"Then why don't you laugh?" Madeleine asked.

"Oh, God," Jonquil said, speaking for the first time.

"You may well ask," Wilde told her.

"Mr. Wilde," Prince Walid said. "I have almost given up trying to fathom the various reasons which so many people seem to have for wishing me dead. I only know that they exist, and that my life is in a constant state of danger. Which is why I take care to be surrounded by good friends."

"I think you want to take a closer look at them," Wilde said.

The Prince nodded. "I do so, from time to time. In your case, I am truly sorry." He smiled. "You make a good cocktail."

"So what happens now?" Wilde asked. "Do I walk the plank?"

"Not for a while, at any rate, Mr. Wilde. You will go with Splendide."

"I was afraid it might come to that." Wilde turned, looked at the large young man. His face still had not changed expression, but his eyes seemed more lively. He carried a pair of handcuffs, and Wilde obligingly held out his wrists. There was nothing else he could do at this moment. He had been taken, for a very long ride, by Carmel Wane and Jonquil Malone. That much was evident. And what was even more aggravating was that, while he had been desperately trying to contact London to find out just what they might be up to, the reason had been staring him in the face all the while.

But committing suicide was not going to get him out of this particular mess. The most vital thing he had learned during his overlong service as Eliminator for Gerald Light was that patience paid, no matter how painful a wait it might involve; patience had once even removed him from the K.G.B. prison outside Moscow, and the art needed no higher testimonial than that.

And this one was going to be painful. He knew it the moment Splendide caught his arms and took them round the back before clicking the handcuffs. "Down there," the young man said.

Wilde went down the circular staircase, swaying with the ship as it rolled, determined not to lose his balance and give them more of a target than they already had. They descended past the dining room to the lower deck, and turned forward. They walked up the corridor and past the cabins and into the forecastle, where there were six bunks and a smell of humanity. Forward of the crew's quarters was another bulkhead door.

"Shades of Captain Bligh," Wilde said. "The chain locker?"

The door was opened, and he was pushed in. The push made him stumble, and of course in the bows the movement of the ship was much greater than anywhere else, as it rose and fell in the gentle swell. His feet caught in the circles of chain and he fell to his knees, attempted to get up, and dropped again. He turned, and sat down on another coil of chain, his back against the bulkhead. Down here there was constant sound, as the swish of water passed the hull.

And he wasn't alone. Splendide had come in behind him, and closed the door. Now he switched on the light. What a large fellow he was. He looked even larger when he was elongated by shadow and standing over his victim. And there was no doubt that Wilde at this moment was his victim.

He clamped his mouth together as firmly as he could, locking his teeth, less to prevent himself from speaking than to preserve the ivories; he had a suspicion that Splendide was not going to be particularly concerned about which bruises showed and which didn't; there was something suggestive about the way he was pulling on a pair of skin-tight leather gloves he had taken from his pocket.

And he was right. Splendide closed his hands together to make one large fist, in a manner with which Wilde was entirely familiar, and then swung it, to and fro. The first blow merely knocked Wilde's head sideways; the second, coming back, caught him while he was still off balance and tumbled him over, into another coil of chain, with his head banging against the skin of the ship. The third blow crashed into his back, above the kidneys, he figured, but extremely unpleasant for his spare ribs. He decided to get up again and managed to take the fourth blow on his right shoulder; it sent him crashing into the chains again. He wasn't sure which hurt more.

Splendide panted, apparently for breath. He unlocked his hands and worked his fingers. "You dumb?"

Wilde had a similar problem in unlocking his jaw. "I soon will be."

"So you have guts." Splendide sounded pleased. "We don't go in for any refined stuff."

"I had gathered that," Wilde said, and tasted blood, seeping into his mouth from the corners of his lip.

"But we get the answers," Splendide said. "Even if you have to shout falsetto."

Presumably that was a threat. "All you have to do is ask," Wilde said.

Splendide frowned. "Come again?"

Wilde swallowed some more blood. "I am perfectly willing to co-operate," he said. "In fact, I am positively anxious. I have been had, and you have been had, and I think we would do better sharing notes."

"So you're a funny fellow as well," Splendide said, and kicked. The canvas deck shoes took Wilde in the belly and doubled him up. At that moment the ship rose to a larger than usual swell, and he could not stop himself tumbling off the coil of chain and on to the deck, at Splendide's feet. And that was the one place he did not wish to be, right this minute.

His teeth hadn't been clamped either, and they rattled most painfully.

"You'll talk when I tell you to," Splendide said. "And it won't be no prepared story."

The door opened. Wilde was very glad to see the extra light. And the people. Madeleine, followed by two of the crew, carrying between them Jonquil Malone. She appeared to be unharmed, but she looked very frightened.

"Welcome," Wilde said, and spat out more blood. "And I never thought I'd be saying that to you."

Madeleine ignored him. "You have not been stupid?" she asked Splendide.

"I have softened him up, a little."

Madeleine closed the door, leaving Jonquil on the other side. Wilde sighed. But she could scarcely hit as hard as her friend.

"You are a British agent," she remarked. "You may as well confess."

"No one has asked me yet," Wilde said. "Or I'd have told them. I am a *retired* British agent."

She seized his hair, jerked his head to and fro. He had never encountered methods quite so primitive before. And for that reason, perhaps, they were surprisingly effective.

"Ow."

"A British agent," she said. "Sent to assassinate the Prince."

"Actually," Wilde confessed when his head had stopped swinging, "I would like to tell you all about it, if you'd give me half a chance."

"Listen," she suggested.

Wilde obeyed. They were getting to him. From the forecastle, even when muted by the sea, there came a noise which could only have been made by Jonquil Malone.

"Difficult to decide whether or not she's enjoying herself," Wilde said.

"She isn't." Madeleine seized his hair again. "It would be best for you to tell the truth."

"For Christ's sake," Wilde said. "No one will let me. You lot are the bloodiest stupidest and most incompetent interrogators I have ever encountered."

She pushed him away from her and he fell over. "Listen," she said.

But this time, apparently, it was up to her; there was no sound from beyond the door. Madeleine jerked her head, and Splendide opened the door. The two sailors outside threw Jonquil Malone in, rather as a double rugby scrum half might throw a long pass. She screamed as she sailed through the air, and Wilde groaned. But there was no escape. She landed on him, all arms and legs, and he gasped for breath.

"Oh, God," she moaned. Her lips were cut, and blood dripped from her chin.

"If you do not tell the truth," Madeleine said, "we shall tear her apart, in front of your eyes."

Jonquil screamed.

"Be my guest," Wilde agreed.

Jonquil screamed again.

"After lunch," Madeleine said. "The Prince is waiting. You think about it." She opened the door. Splendide went with her, switching off the light as he did so.

iii

"Oh, God," Jonquil said, and the anchor chain clanked as she moved.

"What did they do to you?" Wilde asked with interest.

"I suppose, by your lights, they did absolutely nothing," Jonquil said. "Just made me awfully aware that I am a woman. I should imagine that if a man ever touches me again as long as I live I shall go stark raving mad."

"So you *were* enjoying yourself," Wilde said. "I'm glad of that. Because you're not likely to when I can get my hands free."

He could feel her breath on his head as she moved, and he could smell her perfume, even after a dip in the pool. And now some water was scattered on his arm.

"You are," she pointed out, "the most unutterable louse ever to draw breath. When I think that I not only trusted you, I was even a little fond of you, and I certainly supposed you were reasonably competent . . ."

She was so obviously truly distressed that Wilde started to think again.

"Take a deep breath," he said. "And hold it for five seconds. Then tell me what it was Madeleine found in my suitcase that was so incriminating."

There was the sound of heavy breathing from behind him. But whether she was exactly following his instructions he didn't know. "I am going to have a *bruise,*" she said thoughtfully. "The size of a pigeon's egg. Christ, it hurts."

"Where?"

"Mind your own goddamned business."

"Then it is hardly likely to show when you get your clothes on. You were going to tell me something."

"Oh, how the hell do I know what she found in your bloody suitcase," Jonquil demanded. "I always suspected that the British were an overrated race. But to be so goddamned stupid as to carry around some form of identification . . ."

"Do you think, were I quite that stupid, I could have survived twenty years in this business, darling?"

"You are wearing handcuffs," she said, with the voice of a woman who has just remembered where she has left her diamond tiara. "I can scratch your nasty little eyes out. I can pull out all of your hair. I can . . ."

"Try using your apology for a brain," Wilde suggested.

More breathing. By now his eyes were becoming accustomed to the darkness and he could just see her, a long sliver of paleness, sitting next to him. "The last time I was in a position like this," he said, "I was accompanied by two extremely attractive young women, one of whom was positively regal. Strange how the quality of life deteriorates. They got me free, by biting through the rope holding my wrists. Now, I am not suggesting that your teeth are capable of coping with metal, Jonquil darling, but you will descend in my estimation as a woman if you do not have a hairpin tucked away in that auburn mess of yours."

"What do you mean?" she asked. "How do you explain that thing Madeleine was waving around."

"I think it was her own driving licence."

"You have lost me," Jonquil said.

"What a pity I didn't do that a week ago," Wilde said nastily. "We were discussing hairpins."

"For God's sake," she said. "I don't have a hairpin. No one has a hairpin, nowadays. When last did you see a woman with a hairpin?"

"It's not the sort of thing I generally look for, in women. Supposing there was one, do you think you could pick the lock on my handcuffs? In the dark?"

"This is the craziest conversation I have ever heard," she said.

"It's that or a lot of fun and games for you, I think," he reminded her. "Which may put you off women as well as men for a while."

"I can pick a lock," she said. "I was taught how to do that."

"In the dark?"

"Of course in the dark," she shouted. "How many times does one get to pick a lock in the light?"

"There is no need to shout," he said. "Someone may be listening. But you have restored my faith in Israeli Intelligence. No, I'll take that back for the time being. I still have a lot of things on my mind. Now listen very carefully. If you remove my jacket from my shoulders, and tear out the lining, you will find my trusty old safety pin in the hem around the back."

"For God's sake."

"Won't that do?"

"Listen," she said. "Tell me about Madeleine."

"I wish I could," Wilde said. "She grabbed me, escorted me downstairs, and requested me to open our suitcases, so that she could search them all over again. I was quite agreeable, obsequing my way along as I had been instructed, and she produced her stage prop and shouted at the delectable Halma to shoot me. I thought no one was allowed to carry guns around the Prince? Anyway, I had to do something about that."

"And landed us in here," she said bitterly.

"I have an idea we were coming anyway," Wilde said. "If you didn't plant something incriminating in my suitcase, and I don't usually carry anything around with me of my own accord, then Madeleine did the job. She knew just what she was after, too. Jonas Wilde, Eliminator, not Rupert Smart, bartender. Now, doesn't that suggest anything to your fuzzy intelligence?"

"That . . . oh, my God."

"Exactly."

"She's another old acquaintance, and she spotted you right off."

Wilde sighed. "As you told me not very long ago, you can't be very good at your job, or you'd have got further. Coincidences play no part in the business we are in, darling. I found that out a long time ago, and nearly got shot up doing it. Madeleine knew who I was, and who you are, because somebody told her we were coming."

"But who on earth would have done that?"

"Makes you think, I hope. Even you. While you are at that, could you do something about my blazer?"

Her hands ran across his shoulders. "It's not going to be easy," she pointed out. "Tearing the lining out of a blazer while it's still on somebody."

"If it was at all likely to be easy, presumably it wouldn't be necessary. And you don't want to drop the safety pin, either. Because you won't be likely to find it again. Done any thinking yet?"

She pulled the jacket back from his shoulders, and he heard a cautious ripping sound. "Well, there is nobody, is there?" she said. "The whole thing just doesn't make sense. The only people in the whole world who knew we were coming here were Bunty, and Carmel, and . . ."

"Don't stop now," Wilde begged.

The ripping sound suddenly became very loud as the whole inside of the jacket came away.

"But be careful."

"And the man who employs her, and me, and you," Jonquil said. "I don't know who he is. But you are talking the most absolute rubbish, you know. Carmel explained our policy to you. We have to keep the Prince of Xanda alive and happy, for the next fifty years. Aha."

"Got the pin, have you? Oh, good girl. Now prove to me that you aren't as dumb as you look. Because, if you could believe that story you'll believe anything."

"If I am going to pick this lock in the dark," Jonquil said with considerable dignity, "I am going to have to have absolute quiet."

Her breath began to play about his wrists, and she gave a sharp exclamation. Presumably in bending the pin to make the key she had punctured herself. Thus presumably he had had a narrow escape from a similar fate. He remained as still as he could, in view of the heaving of the sea, which seemed to have increased. But he could hear no wind, so obviously they were in the bobble which can usually be found twenty-odd miles south of the French coast, en route to Corsica.

And what was going to happen in Corsica? Or before then. There was not much chance that the Prince of Xanda was going to put into Ajaccio with a couple of would-be assassins on board. He was not, going by the various stories about him, the sort of man who handed people over to the local police. He preferred to deal with them himself.

Now, why did that send shivers up and down his spine? Or was it Jonquil?

And what precisely was he going to do about it all? He was going through the motions at the moment, the motions to which he had been trained, and to which Jonquil had also been trained, presumably. Resist, silently, and break out whenever possible. And then what? There were nine men on board this boat, and two women, and he had got the impression that sexes wouldn't come into it when the action started.

"Got you," Jonquil said. "I'm good at locks. Aren't I good at locks, Jonas?"

"You are an absolute treasure. Now close it up again. But this time don't snap it."

"Don't you *want* to be free?"

"Not until I can use my freedom to some useful purpose. Then I want you to stuff my lining back inside itself so no one can see it's been torn, and pin the pin right in the middle. Think you can manage all of that?"

Her chin bumped into his back. "I could, if they would keep this bloody boat still. Jonas, I still can't make any sense out of what you have been muttering."

"Well, darling, I'll tell you what I have been muttering," Wilde agreed. "Let us suppose for a single instant that there was any truth in the story put out by Carmel Wane, do you seriously suppose that she would employ a murderer who is a total stranger to her? That struck me as odd from the beginning."

"Set a thief to . . ."

"I heard you the first time, and I didn't believe it then. But just let us allow our imagination to wander, and suppose that things are not quite what they seem, that in fact it is the idea of Carmel Wane and her cohorts to rupture the friendly relations which exist between the Prince of Xanda and the West. Just let's suppose, for instance, that they were the ones behind the other assassination attempts, all of which have failed miserably."

"I can't believe that," Jonquil said. "They are . . ."

"My turn," Wilde said. "They must kill the Prince, or come very close to it. And they are at their wits' end, after failure on top of failure, when up pops their dumbest little field agent, one Jonquil Malone, with a photograph and a bead on one Jonas Wilde, assassin, and ex-employee of the British Security Services. A dream come true. He doesn't use weapons. He can be infiltrated right up to the Prince. And then, as Carmel so carefully investigated, he can deliver the goods with but a single blow. Perhaps he might not find escaping as easy as in the past. But does that really matter?"

"You mean you thought of all this while she was talking with you?"

"It's part of my business, darling. Thinking."

"But you went along with it."

"Well, in the first place, the pair of you made it plain that you would be extremely unpleasant if I didn't, and I do hate unpleasantness, and in the second, I suffer from an insatiable curiosity. So Carmel might be able to pull strings and get me slotted in alongside the Prince. As she has done most successfully. But how would she make me kill the man, when I have no desire to do so? There was the problem."

"Oh, my God," Jonquil said.

"Ah. The penny is beginning to drop. Answer, you don't have Wilde kill the Prince, because you know you can't, and because you also know that it isn't necessary. Because Wilde is a killer, he is going to be treated as such by everyone with whom he comes into contact. So all you really need is someone standing beside the Prince, ready to identify the killer, and then, of course, sufficient additional proof to convince the old boy. Because if he is convinced he can only come to one conclusion; none of the other assassins have talked, so he is working in the dark about who is gunning for him. But here at last an identifiable murderer has dropped into his lap. The Eliminator, naturally on a normal assignment for Gerald Light. The British, by God. And that no longer obtains, by itself. The European Community, by God. And would the European Community undertake such a serious venture without at least the tacit approval of Washington, by God? By God, or Allah, as the case may be, but those Western devils are at it again."

"But," Jonquil wondered, "wouldn't that work against the Israelis as well?"

"Of course. I should think that was the whole idea."

"But . . . why should our own people . . . ?" She paused.

"Now you are beginning to see light, dark as it is," Wilde said. "Carmel Wane is not an Israeli, is she? She is a special recruitment, like yourself. And so, no doubt, is her immediate superior. Can you tell me when they appeared on the scene?"

"Well," Jonquil said. "I was seconded to this non-Jewish group about two years ago. We were losing a lot of friends around then, you may remember, and so it was felt that to get maximum efficiency it would be necessary to recruit non-Jews, and let them travel on the passports of their own countries, and fulfil whatever tasks they were assigned to without anyone ever discovering that they were really Israeli agents. It made a lot of sense at the time."

"It still makes a certain amount of sense, providing your recruits are properly screened. So tell me about Carmel Wane."

"I don't know anything about Carmel," she admitted. "I received my instructions from Tel Aviv, as usual, that I was to put myself at the disposal of a group using a certain identification code. That is, I was to put Bunty and me, and the yacht. We were on observation in the Med. A really plush job, as you can imagine. So we waited, and one day Carmel showed up, and used the right code, and informed us that she was our local area commander, and that she would be in touch when she needed us, but for the time being the group was recruiting for a really big mission. She didn't say what, and I didn't expect her to. But she made sure that *Esmeralda* was in good condition."

"That must have been when they discovered that the Prince was having this boat built. And then, by God, you did turn up with a prize, which meant a slight alteration in their plans. For the better, I imagine they decided. But I wonder just how slight an alteration it was. Oops."

There were hands, scrabbling at the bolt on the outside of the door.

"Jonas," she whispered, her voice quavering.

"Sorry, darling," he said. "You are going to have to sit this one out. There is no point in my making a play unless we are certain it is going to succeed."

A moment later the forepeak was bathed in light as the electric bulb glowed. He blinked, and by the time he got his vision straight the door was open, to reveal Madeleine, the young man, Splendide, and two crew members. Wilde sighed. The odds were far too heavy.

"Well," Madeleine said.

"*Malo,*" Wilde said. "There's a hell of a lot of movement up here."

"There'll be more," she said happily. "Come on, Mrs. Smart. We want to have a chat with you."

"Again?" Wilde asked. "Can't you do it here?"

Madeleine smiled; her lips drew back from her teeth in a gesture reminiscent of a snarling dog. Correction, he thought—bitch.

"The Prince has a sadistic streak," she said. "Especially about women."

"Jonas," Jonquil begged.

"Think about something else," Wilde suggested, and a moment later she was gone, plucked through the doorway by the two men.

Splendide remained for a moment, gazing at Wilde thoughtfully. Perhaps he'll beat me up again, Wilde thought hopefully. But the moment wasn't right. There were too many people around. And anyway, Splendide wasn't thinking of coming closer. He went outside and closed the door behind himself. The light went off.

And Wilde began to sweat. How much could Jonquil take? How much would she have to take? And what would happen when she blurted out what they had been discussing? He couldn't make up his mind whether that would be advantageous or not. Much would depend upon how much influence the woman Madeleine had with the Prince, how far he would go in believing everything that she had to say.

And there was a realm about which he didn't have a clue, Wilde realised.

Meanwhile there were problems. Mainly heat. It was afternoon by now, and the sun beating on the deck above had turned the forepeak into an oven. He slipped the handcuffs and wiped his face from time to time, but he didn't dare remove his jacket, just in case someone came in unexpectedly.

And then, it was a long time since breakfast. He wondered who had tasted the Prince's lunch. Probably the girl Halma, again. Poor Halma. But she had assisted Madeleine in his cabin. Because she was with Madeleine when the lid blew off, or because she was obeying orders from the Prince's security chief? The fact was, he and the Prince were equally in the dark about who could be trusted and who couldn't on board this boat.

And even more than the hunger was the thirst. His mouth seemed to be stuck firmly to his tongue.

And worse than any of those was the thought of what might be happening to Jonquil Malone. She had been gone for well over an hour. But was even Jonquil what she seemed? He would have bet his bottom dollar on that. Which was just as well, he reflected, because he had certainly just bet his life.

And now the ship was slowing. He sat up. But the engine beat had definitely changed as the revolutions had been reduced. And there were feet thumping on the deck above him. He did some very hasty calculations. It was about seven hours since they left St. Tropez. Say fourteen knots. Maybe a shade more. They would be off the west coast of Corsica, all right. But they could hardly have reached Ajaccio as yet. Which meant that they were about to enter one of the many coves and inlets and bays which serrate the western coast of the island. Which meant that they were about to anchor.

To anchor? Wilde leapt to his feet and flattened himself against the bulkhead, almost at the very moment that the chain started to move. It whipped up from the floor in a long flow of scraping metal, dislodged dust and rust to fill his nostrils, brushing one leg with effortless violence, cascading out of the hawse-pipe while sweat cascaded down Wilde's face. Two seconds ago he had been sitting on top of that lot. What would have happened if he hadn't moved when he did? Presumably much would have depended on whether any of the coils had got themselves wrapped around his arms or legs.

At the very best something would have been shattered beyond repair. At the worst he would have wound up with his head in the hawse-pipe, being mangled to death most unpleasantly.

Had somebody planned that?

But the anchor was now plunged into the clear blue waters of the bay, and the chain was coming to rest. He could hear orders above him; slacken a little. Some more chain was eased out. He did not dare move until they were happy with the situation up there. But now the feet were retreating. Wilde took several very long breaths. He had been angry earlier. But he was a lot angrier now. There was a surge of really vicious hatred coursing through his veins and muscles, the sort of thing his trainers had spent so many months installing into his system, and which he had spent so much time attempting to get rid of. But it was still there, thank God.

And now there were feet in the forecastle, and hands on the bolt. They were coming in to discover what was left of him, if anything. Wilde moved forward, seized the handle of the door, and as the bolt was slipped and the person outside pushed, he pulled with all his strength.

PART TWO

The Man Who Killed Men

CHAPTER 6

The sailor shot through the air, his feet leaving the ground before he could release the outside handle. As he passed, Wilde threw both arms around his waist, and swung him round; the man's head made a sickening crunch as it slammed into the bulkhead. His body went limp, but he had not been alone. Another sailor stood behind him, his mouth dropping open in dismayed surprise at what was happening. Wilde handed him the unconscious man as forcefully as he could manage. The sailor instinctively brought up his hands to grasp the unwanted gift, and Wilde ducked, seized him in turn around the knees, and upended the pair of them. The second man's head hit the edge of a bunk as he went down, and he lay still once he reached the deck.

Back to square one. But whereas the last time he had been uncertain as to just what he was doing, now he was in no doubt at all. The cold fury continued to course up and down his nerves.

The forecastle was empty, and of weapons as well. But there had to be weapons somewhere on board this ship. The door to the corridor stood open, and the corridor was deserted. Wilde stepped through, opened the door to Captain Albarana's cabin. This too was empty, but there were drawers and cupboards. Wilde tore them open, angrily, found nothing he could use. The cabin beyond was his own, tidily empty, and the suitcases had been restored to their proper places beneath the lower bunk. Opposite was the girl Halma's room. Nothing there, either.

He stood in the lobby at the foot of the circular staircase, and listened. From above there came the clink of glasses, and some laughter. For suddenly the engines had stopped, and the whole ship was quiet, save for the hum of the generator. And the Prince was celebrating a safe landfall. Wilde opened the bulkhead door to the engine room, found himself in the first place in another lobby, which contained the deep freeze and the central heating boiler and acted as a buffer between the heat and noise of the engine room and the crew's quarters.

He opened the next door, stood on the catwalk between the two huge diesels, and paused to admire them. They were superb pieces of equipment, and in superb condition. Whichever side Captain Albarana was on, he knew his engines, and he knew how to treat them. And his tools, which were what Wilde was really looking for. Aft of the engines was the generator, and aft of the engine room itself was yet another lobby, and this was the tool room; one bulkhead was entirely lined with gleaming stainless steel spanners, varying in size from slivers of metal scarcely longer than a man's hand to great things about the length of a human forearm.

He tested them for balance, took off his torn blazer, and placed five of the spanners in the belt of his pants. Now he could listen again, for now he was right aft, beneath the owner's stateroom, he figured, from the immense layer of sound-proofing which stretched across the deck above his head. But even farther aft there was a ladder, leading up through a narrow space between the stern and, he hoped, the deck. A way out. And one which could be used to maximum effect.

He listened to a noise from forward. A shouting and a banging. Someone had gone into the forecastle.

Wilde began to climb, quickly, hand over hand on the iron rungs, his feet making no sound in their rubber-soled deck shoes. It was a long way up, past the cabin deck to arrive beneath a hatch, presumably the one over which Jonquil had stumbled as they had come on board. Was it only this morning?

The hatch was unbolted; there was no suggestion of bad weather and here was a quick way down to the bowels of the ship. He paused, to make sure of his breathing and to listen some more. There was some agitation from above him now, as well, voices raised and angry orders being given. But it was all in a foreign tongue, presumably Arabic.

And now there came a shout from beneath him. He looked down, removing the smallest of the five spanners from his belt as he did so. A man stared up at him, shouting, uncertain that it was the fugitive in the dim light. Wilde let the spanner go, putting all his power in his shoulder behind it. It was not possible to miss, in the confined space, especially as the man looking up did not realise there was anything coming down until it hit him. The noise was more a squelch rather than a thud, and was followed by a clump at the foot of the ladder.

Time to move. The odds were narrowing every moment. Wilde sucked air into his lungs, threw open the hatch, and leapt out, grabbing the spanners from his belt as he did so. There had indeed been the beginnings of a cocktail party on the after deck. The table was filled with glasses, and the chairs with the Prince of Xanda and the woman Madeleine. The man, Splendide, was just moving, together with Captain Albarana, towards the door into the swimming saloon. At the sound of the crashing hatch they turned to face the trouble, and saw the spanners scything through the air. Knife throwing had been included in Wilde's training. Splendide side-stepped the first flailing piece of steel but took the second in the middle of the chest. He stepped backwards and fell over the raised doorstep into the saloon, and the third spanner whistled over his head and took Captain Albarana on the point of the jaw. He hit the deck without a sound.

Wilde paused for breath, and to smile at the Prince and the woman. The Prince had put on a white shirt over green and orange striped Bermuda shorts, and sandals; Madeleine wore all of her bikini. They were therefore obviously unarmed, and Wilde still possessed the largest spanner.

"How nice," he remarked. "This part of Corsica has always contained my favourite anchorages."

For he had recognised where they were; all around them were the empty red cliffs of the Corsican coast, except to the west, where lay the open sea; they had entered the huge Gulf of Porto, and were anchored in one of the many coves which extend inland, still in deep water, he calculated, and all alone; there were no boats to be seen and this stretch of coast could only be reached overland by mule. The Prince had chosen a magnificently secluded place to spend the night.

"It seems as if you were right, Madeleine." The Prince spoke calmly and did not appear to be deeply disturbed. Unlike the woman, who gripped the arms of her chair and stared at Wilde as if he were a snake and she a rabbit. "This man is dangerous. And even successful. Do you mean to kill me, Mr. Smart? Or should I call you Mr. Wilde?"

Wilde went closer; there were feet on the stairs, and a moment later the two remaining members of the crew emerged, one with his arm in a sling from his earlier encounter with Wilde; they were accompanied by Bruno the chef and Halma. Halma carried her pistol.

"I'd rather not," Wilde said, and sat next to the Prince. "But if that young lady doesn't put away that gun I may have to."

The Prince looked at the spanner, resting only a foot from the side of his head.

"Do not shoot, Halma," he said.

"And tell your policemen to go away," Wilde said. "They can take the captain and Splendide with them, and resuscitate them. And Bruno, it has been a long day. Do you think you could make me a sandwich? Two sandwiches, as a matter of fact, and a long cold glass of rum and Coca-Cola, to restore the battered tissues."

Bruno gaped at him.

"Perhaps you would be so kind, Excellency," Wilde suggested.

The Prince snapped his fingers, and Bruno snapped to attention. "*Si, si,*" he said. "*Prego.*" He disappeared behind the two men carrying the captain. Halma continued to stare at them, but she had returned the pistol to the pocket of her apron.

"Come and sit down, Halma," Wilde suggested. "And I will have the gun."

Halma hesitated, and then approached. "I cannot sit in the presence of . . . of Mr. Watt," she said.

"I'm sure he won't mind," Wilde said, "as this is a very special occasion."

Halma gazed at the Prince, who nodded briefly.

"The gun," Wilde said. "Butt first, or His Excellency gets a dented skull."

Halma drew the little pistol from her pocket, reversed it, and gave it to Wilde.

"There's just one thing more," he said. "Would you bolt the hatch aft?" He held the pistol in his right hand, left the spanner on his lap. Halma bolted the hatch in place, and then returned to the table. She sat opposite Wilde, her back to the saloon and the forward part of the ship. She acted as a buffer in front of the Prince. For the moment at any rate there was no possibility of surprise.

"Why do you not shoot me and get it over with?" the Prince asked.

"Because I don't mean to shoot you at all," Wilde said. "My difficulty may lie in convincing you of that. But first I must ask you one or two questions. I was told you do not allow guns in your immediate vicinity."

"Halma is specially privileged," the Prince said.

"I'm sure. Then where are the rest of the weapons on board this ship?"

"There are none, Mr. Wilde. I give you my word."

"Um. Let's try something else. Where is Miss Malone?"

"Miss Malone?"

"He means the Irish woman, Master," Halma said.

"Ah," the Prince said. "She is in my cabin."

"Having what done to her?"

"She will be all right," the Prince said. "I do not think she has been permanently affected. She is presently resting."

"And was your treatment effective?"

"After a little while, yes," the Prince said. "She confessed to being an Israeli agent. She confessed to your being a British agent, as well."

"And this one?" Wilde glanced at Madeleine, who still had not moved.

"She did not mention her at all. But after a little while she stopped giving us information. We are letting her sleep."

"You are so kind," Wilde said. "And what do you make of what she said?"

The Prince shrugged. "It but confirms what I have long been told by my advisers, but refused to believe. That the Israelis are not to be trusted. And as you are involved as well, Mr. Wilde, it seems that the entire political structure on which I have built my policies cannot be trusted. I will have to think again. Nor will killing me have any effect, now. There are many in my country who wish to reverse my principles, who see in me a traitor to my race."

"And that doesn't make you think?" Wilde asked. "You must admit, Excellency, that whether or not the Western countries can be trusted, they are not exactly run by fools. Why should they do anything to break up their relationship with Xanda, when it is such a fruitful one for both sides?"

"Believe me, Mr. Wilde, that is a question I have been asking myself since your arrest. Without finding any answers."

"Because there aren't any," Wilde said. "In that direction. This is what we call a put-up job, Excellency. I was inveigled on board under a false pretence too absurd to waste time on, the idea being that as soon as I was on board I should be revealed for what I am, an executioner for the British Government."

"You mean you do not deny that?" the Prince asked with great interest.

"No, sir, but I was not sent to kill you. It would be very helpful if you'd try believing that. But of course, once my identity is revealed, once it is discovered that I am a British agent working for the Israelis, I do not have to kill you, do I, from the point of view of the people who set this up. The mere fact of my presence is sufficient to accomplish the rupture in diplomatic relations that they seek. And it would seem that they have succeeded. The point is, of course, that I am not supposed to be alive to talk about it. Madeleine instructed Halma to shoot me, the moment she decided to make her play." He winked at the Xandan girl. "But Halma missed."

The Prince stared at him for several seconds. "You are a very bold man, Mr. Wilde. I suppose, to be an assassin, one has to be, very bold. You are also a very shrewd one. But perhaps I also am shrewd. It was my command that you not be killed, immediately following your arrest. Certainly Madeleine wished to do this." His eyes moved to look at Madeleine. "What do you say about it, dear one?"

Madeleine drew a long breath. "I would say it is a very carefully prepared cover story," she said. "As you have just said, Excellency, this man is at once bold and clever. He is the best in his field. He is known as the most dangerous man in the world."

The Prince smiled. "The most dangerous man in the world. I like that. But it seems I am in an impasse, Mr. Wilde. Madeleine says you have been sent here to kill me, and you do not deny that is your usual function. On the other hand, you have not used this opportunity, when you would seem to hold all the high cards, as you have just about liquidated my crew, and there are surely sufficient bullets in that pistol to dispose of the three of us here, and the tender waiting alongside for you to depart for the shore. This is mystifying. But I still cannot be sure that it is not some part of a still deeper plan, as you have produced no proof that Madeleine is anything better than she claims to be, my most faithful and loving mistress. It would be very helpful if you could supply something more positive than theories."

Wilde glanced from him to the woman. He hadn't really had the time to do a great deal of thinking about it. Or perhaps while he had had the time he had not really had the inclination.

Then he remembered something. He took his eyes away from the Prince long enough to have a look around the bay in which they were anchored. To the left the cliffs were hardly more than a hundred feet away, and sheer; to the right they were over half a mile distant; and in front of *Female Spirit* they were once again about half a mile off. But closer than that, descending into the water like a wedge of cheese two hundred yards away, there was a spit of land protruding from the left, conveniently forming and concealing a smaller bay beyond. And fitting his theory? It was certainly worth a gamble. There was too much at stake not to take the risk.

"I will prove it to you, Excellency," he said. "I joined your ship this morning, as you may recall, and to the best of my knowledge neither I nor Miss Malone was ever told of our destination."

"So?" the Prince asked.

But Madeleine was frowning.

"I am assuming that you did tell Madeleine where you planned to make your first stop?"

"She suggested it. She knows the Mediterranean much better than I."

"Ah," Wilde said. "Well, then, I would say that you will find, awaiting just beyond that headland over there, snugly out of sight from here, a motor cruiser called *Esmeralda*. It will have on board a crew who are waiting to hear from Madeleine, here, either that I have succeeded or that I have been killed in the attempt, and either way that the fat is in the fire as far as Israel's relations with Xanda are concerned. And one of the crew, I am prepared to bet my bottom dollar, is a tall blond woman with the disposition of a rattlesnake."

The Prince glanced at Madeleine. Some of the colour had gone from her cheeks, but she continued to stare at Wilde in a most venomous fashion. Two of a kind, he thought.

"Halma," the Prince said. "Take the tender and see if you can find the ship of which Mr. Wilde speaks."

"But don't be obvious about it, Halma," Wilde said. "Pretend to be joyriding. Take a sweep around the whole bay, staying well out, and just cast a casual glance into that cove as you go."

Halma nodded, got up, and went down the accommodation ladder. A moment later the outboard spluttered into life. Wilde noted once again that Halma was a very efficient young woman.

"How do you know of this?" the Prince asked Wilde.

"I don't *know* of it," Wilde admitted. "But the ship I have in mind is the one that brought Miss Malone and me to St. Tropez, and then left again in a great hurry."

"Ah. Yes, that is good. Because it could not possibly have left on any instructions from you. Yes, that is good." The Prince smiled. "Your sandwiches, Mr. Wilde."

Bruno was opening the saloon door very cautiously. He carried a tray on which there were four attractive-looking sandwiches, and the glass of rum and Coca-Cola Wilde had requested.

"I am sure you must be both hungry and thirsty," the Prince remarked, continuing to smile.

Bruno set the sandwiches on the table, bowed, and withdrew.

"So have one," Wilde suggested.

The Prince gazed at him for several seconds.

"And a drink," Wilde said. "You have also had a rather busy day."

The Prince's smile returned. "I think we will allow Madeleine to enjoy that privilege."

Her gaze switched from Wilde to the Prince. "You are beginning to believe this man," she said.

"I am waiting for proof," the Prince said. "Eat, my dear one. And wash it down with a swallow from the drink." His smile died. "You would not disappoint me?"

Madeleine slowly took a sandwich, bit into it, masticated it for some seconds, and swallowed. She gasped for breath, and drank some of the rum and Coke.

The Prince reached up and snapped his fingers, and Bruno reappeared.

"I think you should bring another drink for Mr. Wilde," he said. "I have changed my mind. And Bruno, you will be tasting this one."

Madeleine stared at him, her mouth slowly opening. "You . . . you bastard," she said, and reached for her throat. But before she could make it the strength seemed to leave her muscles, and she subsided into the chair, hands hanging limp, body flaccid.

"By God," Wilde said. "You make me feel like an amateur."

"Bruno is very enthusiastic," the Prince agreed. "His sole idea is to protect me. I think he is going to be a success. Ah, Bruno, would you be so kind?"

Bruno waggled his moustaches at Wilde, and sipped the drink, then placed the glass on the table.

"That should reassure you," the Prince said. "And the sandwiches are quite all right."

Wilde scratched his head. "Is she dead?"

"Ah, no. That would have been a waste, certainly before we knew what Halma has to tell us. But she is here now."

The outboard was chattering next to the yacht, and a moment later it died. Halma appeared at the top of the ladder.

"Well?" asked the Prince.

"There is no yacht in the anchorage, Master," she said.

The Prince sighed. "Now there is a great pity, Mr. Wilde, I was growing to like you."

"But there are people, Master," Halma said. "A tent, by the shore. I could not see how many people. But one of them was a blond woman."

ii

"That is hardly conclusive," the Prince said.

"It's worth a look," Wilde argued. "Believe me, Excellency, you don't usually get company around here. It's too remote. Just for example, you can't reach it by car."

"So you would say they were dropped by their yacht, which then left," the Prince said thoughtfully. "Of course. Because either you or Miss Malone might have released the name *Esmeralda* under interrogation. Will you work for me, Mr. Wilde?"

"I have reservations about that," Wilde said. "I'd like to see just what you have done to Jonquil Malone first. But I was employed to keep you alive, officially. I will continue to do that."

The Prince considered, and then nodded. "That is fair enough. Now, the people beyond the headland. We shall have them arrested?"

"How?" Wilde asked.

The Prince frowned. "Undoubtedly they are my enemies."

"Undoubtedly," Wilde said. "But only we know that. I think you would have a hard time proving it to the satisfaction of the French police."

The Prince stroked his beard. "I am Walid of Xanda."

"I'm sure you are," Wilde agreed. "But that also would have to be proved. At the very least there would be a considerable amount of publicity attached to the whole thing. And would your own people really like to think of you gallivanting around the Mediterranean in a luxury yacht while they are sweating it out under the Xandan sun?"

"Bah," the Prince said. "My people do as they are told." He got up impatiently, went to the rail, and looked down at the dark blue of the sea. "But I know how we can prove it." He snapped his fingers, and Bruno appeared in the doorway. "How much did you give her?"

"No more than a drop, sir," Bruno said. "Just to disarm the gentleman, was the idea." His eyes were attempting to apologise to Wilde.

"Wake her up, Halma," the Prince commanded.

Halma thrust her fingers into Madeleine's hair, raised her head from the table, and slapped the little woman twice on the cheek, very hard. All without changing her expression. Wilde wondered what *would* change Halma's expression.

Madeleine groaned, and her eyelids flickered.

"I am waiting, Halma," the Prince said.

Halma leaned over Madeleine, moved her hair to one side, bent closer, and sank her remarkably white teeth into the lobe of Madeleine's ear. Madeleine's head jerked, her eyes spread wide, and a trickle of blood dropped on to her shoulder.

"Oh, God," she gasped.

Halma stood up, and wiped her mouth.

Wilde scratched his head.

The Prince leaned against the rail. "Mr. Wilde has convinced me that you are a traitor, Madeleine," he said softly. "Which must mean that you have been betraying me for some time. That every time you have shared my bed it was with hate in your heart and not love. I think I find that hardest of all to forgive."

Madeleine's right hand slowly crept up to her ear. She stared at the Prince.

"Now I want you to tell me who are the people camped just beyond the headland. Exactly where Mr. Wilde said they would be. I would also like to know their plans."

Madeleine glanced at Wilde, and licked her lips. "Exactly where *he* said they would be, Walid," she whispered.

The Prince smiled. "That will not work, any longer. If indeed his mission was to kill me, then he would already have accomplished it and made his escape. That is a point you cannot explain away. He has very efficiently demolished the major part of my crew. There is really nothing to stop him doing it. Now, I will tell you what *I* am going to do. I am going to put to sea, in a little while. We are going to cruise very slowly towards the Balearics. That is a long way. Over two hundred miles. When we wake up tomorrow morning we shall be out of sight of land or other ships. We shall be alone in the middle of the Mediterranean Sea. Then I am going to stop the ship, and I am going to tie a rope around your waist, and trail you over the stern." The smile grew more terrible. "But immediately before I do that I shall empty some offal over the side as well. You will enjoy your swim, Madeleine. The water will be warm, and the weather forecast is good, so it should also be calm. And we will stand up here and look at you, and no doubt you will splash about down there and look at us. For a while."

As he spoke the colour slowly drained from Madeleine's face, but she did not move.

"Alternatively," the Prince said, "you can co-operate with me, and tell me about your friends, and I will merely have you strangled. Better yet, Madeleine, as it is you we are discussing, I will strangle you myself. With these very hands which you have pretended to enjoy when they caressed your body. Perhaps you will pretend to enjoy them then as well. But I do promise you that it will be quicker than the sharks. Less traumatic, perhaps."

Madeleine licked her lips. And Wilde wanted to do the same. Because there could be no doubt that Walid meant every word he was saying. He glanced at Halma. She had, naturally, not changed expression. But she was gazing at Madeleine almost benignly, as a cat might regard the mouse which was soon going to be offered for its dinner.

"I don't know who is encamped round there," Madeleine whispered. "Or what they intend. I was merely instructed to give your destination as soon as I learned it myself."

The Prince continued to smile. "I had supposed you would adopt that attitude, you know. Ah, well, I have never seen someone eaten by sharks. And I believe that one should try to see everything, experience everything, in this life."

Madeleine's fingers were eating into the arms of her chair. "It is the truth," she said. "I swear it. By Christ, I swear it."

"Who did you give this information to?" Wilde asked.

Her head turned, but she would not look at him. "A man in St. Tropez. Last night."

"Which man?" But it could not have been Bunty, of course; they had still been at sea.

"A man called Steve. That is all I know."

"But you know who you work for," Wilde said.

Now her head did turn and she gazed at him.

"I think you should tell Mr. Wilde, Madeleine," the Prince said. "Otherwise I will give you to Splendide for an hour. She does not like Splendide, you know, Mr. Wilde. She regards him as an abomination."

"I work for a man called Leigh," Madeleine said.

"You can't stop there," Wilde said. "Tell us about Mr. Leigh."

She shrugged. "It is his task, to destroy the rapport between Xanda and the West. By killing the Prince, was the original intention. But as that has not proved possible, he started to think of other ways."

"Yet managed to infiltrate you right into the Prince's entourage."

"Into my bed, Mr. Wilde," Walid reminded him. "She was good in bed. I have hardly known better. And she was only acting. That is . . ."

"Unforgivable," Wilde said. "You mentioned that. Don't let's put her off. If Leigh could get you right up to the Prince, why couldn't you do the killing?"

"It was not in my contract," she said. "Besides, what was I to kill him with? He may have pretended to be fond of me, but he still had me searched after every time I left the palace."

"So maybe you were trying to love him to death."

"I do not find her amusing, Mr. Wilde," the Prince said. "Or what she tried to do. If you are going to work for me, you will kindly show a proper respect."

"Ah," Wilde said. "But I am not going to work for you, am I, Prince Walid? I don't like your attitudes, very much. I think they show an unnecessarily sadistic streak."

The Prince stared at him in genuine surprise.

"No one can speak to the Master like that," Halma said. "You must die."

"We all must die, sweetheart," Wilde said. "But only his nibs is really likely to do that soon. Unless I look after him."

"You have a very high opinion of yourself, Mr. Wilde," Walid remarked.

"No, sir," Wilde said. "Of my capabilities. But you don't suppose that things are going to rest here, do you? Madeleine, what were you supposed to do when you got here?"

"I don't know what you mean," she muttered.

"Weren't you supposed to contact your friends if something went wrong, or inform them if everything was going according to plan?"

"Only, if possible, to let them know where we were bound," she said.

"What reason can they have for trailing us, Mr. Wilde?" asked the Prince. "If in some way they are thinking of assaulting my yacht, Madeleine would know of it."

"Now that I wonder," Wilde said. "Because she might not have been prepared to accept the job. Do you know what your friends are planning, Madeleine?"

She shook her head. "I swear it."

"Bah," said the Prince. "Let me give her to Splendide. Bruno, get Splendide up here. He'll soon have her singing a different tune."

"I swear it," Madeleine shrieked, suddenly coming to life and trying to get up. Halma pushed her back into the chair. "They told me to make sure Wilde got the job, and then to accuse him once we had got to sea. That is all. They said they would keep an eye on things. That is all. I swear it."

"Bruno," the Prince said.

"Alas, Excellency," Bruno said, looking truly distressed, "Splendide is not feeling so good, Excellency. His rib, it is broken."

"Well, where is the captain?"

"His jaw is broken, Excellency."

The Prince frowned. "And my crew?"

"One has a broken jaw, also, Excellency. One has a dislocated shoulder. And two have concussion. But . . ." He brightened. "Zahir is all right. He is only slightly bruised."

"You are certainly a potent enemy, Mr. Wilde," the Prince said. "And now I hope you will prove to be a potent friend. Can you tell me what we should do now?"

"You have two choices, Excellency," Wilde said. "One is to go round to Ajaccio, abandon your yacht there, and catch the first available plane back to Xanda. If you do that, you will solve your immediate problem. On the other hand, these people will resume laying their plans. And one day they are going to succeed. The other is to carry the fight to them."

iii

The Prince plucked at his beard as he gazed at Wilde. "Carry the fight to them," he said. "By all that is holy, I like the sound of that. Explain what you mean, Mr. Wilde."

"I mean that, as we are here, and they are there, just beyond that headland, and as they do not yet know what has been happening on board *Female Spirit,* they are likely to stay there at least until tomorrow. But it also occurs to me that if Madeleine here recommended this place as a good stopover, they may have some other plan in mind. I think we should hit them first. So far as we know there are only two people in that camp. And I have a pretty good idea of who one of them is likely to be. I think, as soon as it's dark, and it is going to be dark in an hour or so, we might be able to carry out an old British custom, and cut them out."

"Cut them out? I do not understand."

"I mean go ashore, take them prisoner, and bring them back here. Once that is accomplished, *Female Spirit* can indeed put to sea, and once out in the middle of the Mediterranean, as you pointed out just now, you can obey your own laws."

"A magnificent conception," the Prince said. "I grow to like you, more and more, Mr. Wilde. I will have you work for me. On this I am determined. But we will discuss that later. How many men will you need?"

"I suspect events are going to be conditioned by how many men I have got," Wilde said. He glanced at Halma instinctively.

She nodded. "I will help, Master."

"I thought you might," Wilde said.

"And you will be able to manage with just the girl?" the Prince asked.

"I should think so."

"But I foresee one problem, Master," Halma said. "Mr. Wilde's plan is to take *Female Spirit* to sea, afterwards. But with Captain

Albarana and four members of the crew out of action, I do not see how we are going to do that."

"I will sail your ship for you," Wilde said. "I will need help in that direction also, however, and that will have to come from Jonquil Malone. I propose to investigate that help now. And you had better hope that she is a good physical state. And in good mental condition also."

The Prince nodded thoughtfully. "Then let us go to her. Halma, you will bring Madeleine."

Halma stood up, tapped Madeleine on the shoulder. The woman, who had been listening intently to the conversation, seemed to jerk into full consciousness, and got to her feet.

"I am sure that there is much more valuable information she can give us," the Prince said. "As we have an hour to waste, it might be a good idea to question her further."

"You really have a limited potential for enjoyment," Wilde pointed out. "I only work on one condition; I run the operation. The entire operation, Excellency. Starting from now."

The Prince led him through the saloon and down the spiral staircase. "I had gained the impression that you were running the entire operation from some minutes ago, Mr. Wilde. I was merely trying to be helpful. Ah, well, when it is done, no doubt you will allow them all to be my prisoners?"

Wilde considered. But there was not a hell of a lot of alternative. "Let's have a look at Jonquil," he said.

The Prince led him aft, through the dining saloon and into a lobby carpeted in green and white. There were two double cabins on either side, and a fifth door in the centre. This led to the master cabin. Perhaps the royal suite would have been more accurate, Wilde thought. It spread the full width of the ship, of course, which made it, even by the standards which could be applied to a house, a large room. His memory of the exterior of the ship told him that there were no windows down here, only ports, and these were covered by heavy green and white drapes, but the soft current of air propelled by the fans removed the slightest tendency to claustrophobia.

There was a dressing table on the starboard bulkhead, and the port bulkhead was all hanging locker space. Forward on the port side was a door to the royal bathroom. The rest of the cabin seemed entirely occupied by bed, some eight feet long and ten feet wide, an enormous expanse of green and white pillow and sheet, reflecting endlessly from the mirror which covered the deck head. That was predictable enough.

What had not been predictable was the appearance of Jonquil Malone. She was scattered in the centre of the softness, and seemed to belong to the roof. And scattered was a very apt description, Wilde realised. Her hair was spread, and so were her legs; she lay on her side, and might have been taking a very long and very high hurdle, as her toes seemed to be trying to reach each corner at the same time. Her arms were similarly outflung, and her face was half turned into the sheets, moving slightly as she breathed. She sweated, and sighed. She was the classic picture of the sleeping woman, after . . .

Wilde turned his head, slowly, to look at the Prince. "What did you do to her?"

Walid smiled. "I made love to her, Mr. Wilde."

Wilde scratched his head. "I have an idea I am starting to dislike you, Excellency," he said. "Just that?"

"Oh, come now, Mr. Wilde," Walid said. "When I make love to a woman, it is never, just that."

"That thought is occurring to me. Can you tell me why she is so totally out?"

"Ah, well, you see," the Prince said, stroking his beard, "she was a little nervous, at the beginning. It is a remarkable fact, but most women are, when I invite them into my bed. So I gave her a little medicine that I carry about with me, which overcomes the inhibitions, relaxes the muscles, fills the brain with erotic thoughts and visions. Of course, it also has a slight sedative effect."

"You mean you made love to her when she was out?"

The Prince looked shocked. "Oh no, no, Mr. Wilde, where would the pleasure be in that? She was very awake and conscious. But as I say, the effects of the drug are to a certain extent sedative, and the effects of my own techniques are certainly exhausting, and the two combined to make her very sleepy."

"You," Wilde said, "are a liar."

The Prince shrugged. "Perhaps I could demonstrate my art," he said. "We could use Halma. We have an hour to waste."

Wilde scratched his head some more. "I think erotic displays should be saved for the completion of our mission."

"As you wish."

"But I hope you will have no objection to my attempting to revive Miss Malone?"

"It would be better for her to sleep."

"Why?"

"I think you should take my word for that."

"I'm not in a word-taking mood. Besides, I would like to know that I have someone I can trust backing me up, if you follow me. No reflection on yourself, Excellency."

The Prince shrugged again. "Enjoy yourself, Mr. Wilde. I will go and see how Halma is doing with Madeleine, and I suppose I should go and look at the men you so savagely mistreated. No doubt you will inform me when you wish to make preparations for our departure."

"Eh?"

"I meant, our raid on these people."

"You keep using the word our."

The Prince smiled. "I wish to come with you, Mr. Wilde. In fact I insist upon it."

"Now just look here," Wilde said.

"I am every bit as expert as Halma, I do promise you."

"I'm sure you're an expert at everything, Excellency. But my job is to look after you. Not expose you to every possible risk."

"The decision is mine, surely," Walid pointed out. "As you made clear to me just now, these people have been after my blood for four years. Once or twice they have come very close to achieving their object. Indeed, they would have done so by now had they not underestimated your fearsome abilities. I wish to be in at the death, so to speak. I am not convinced that even you and Halma, and she is a very capable girl, will be able to cope. There could well be three people against you."

Wilde shook his head.

"Listen, Mr. Wilde," Walid said. "Have you any idea what it is like, to be sheikh of a country like Xanda? Do you think it is all fun and games?"

Wilde looked at the unconscious girl on the bed. "You seem to have your moments."

"Bah. A woman? I have had a woman every day of my life since I was thirteen. It is the law. The Prince must be above all men, better than all men. So I cheat a little, with my drug. For the rest, it is a matter of business, not pleasure. It has been so since I was a boy. A matter of looking at life through other men's eyes. At least my father once commanded his own army into battle. Even that pleasure is denied me. Now, for the first time, and I suppose the last time in my life, I have the opportunity. I am not asking to lead this army. I have seen you at work, Mr. Wilde. I will be proud to serve under you. But I will come with you if I have to go on my own. Or if I have to beg for the privilege."

Wilde scratched his head some more. "I suppose, if you put it that way . . . but you'll obey orders."

"Of course, Mr. Wilde. I will do everything you say."

Wilde nodded. "Okay. Now, if you will permit me some time alone with Miss Malone?"

The Prince shrugged. "It would be better to let her awake in her own time, Mr. Wilde. However, I will wish you good fortune."

He closed the door. How quiet it was down here. Because this cabin was sound-proofed within the general sound-proofing of the ship, he realised. He could not even hear the gentle lapping of the water. A place where the Prince could shut himself away, with his woman of the day, and know he was alone. What a character. What a horrible character. And yet, what a fascinating one as well.

Wilde went into the bathroom, found a sponge, soaked it in cold water, and returned with a towel to the bed. He climbed into the middle, knelt beside Jonquil, raised her head, and inserted the towel beneath it, and then squeezed water on to her face. She sighed, and rolled over violently, arms and legs flying, and smiled in her sleep.

Wilde soaked the sponge again, and tried again. Her eyelids flickered.

The third time her eyes actually opened for a moment before shutting again. But she was awake. Her fingers slid up his arms and round his neck, and she pulled his head down to hers, and then positively threw it away from her.

"Ugh," she said, sitting up. "You're not the Master."

Wilde did some more head scratching. "I never thought I was, sweetheart. But I try."

She propelled herself up the bed, away from him, scooping hair from her eyes, reaching to the bedside table for her glasses. "You . . . you didn't . . . ?"

"I like mine awake," he said. "But I really wouldn't have thought it would trouble you."

"Don't touch me," she said. "Just don't touch me. I mean, you're very sweet, Jonas, and I love you dearly, but right this minute . . ."

"You are totally satisfied. That figures. I wasn't going to touch you, as a matter of fact. I just wanted to make sure that you were all right. I had envisaged the most terrible fate overtaking you. But it seems things are worse than I thought."

"Oh, you are such a funny man," she said coldly. "I think we were quite wrong about the Prince."

"We were?"

"He is very charming. He explained that it was all a misunderstanding, and that he wanted to make it up to me. If he could."

"And after hours of endeavour he succeeded."

She had on her spider-spotting stare. "He was a perfect gentleman. He thought we should be alone, and so he brought me down here. Isn't it marvellous?"

"Just super, darling. But you had been here before, hadn't you? During your medical examination?"

"Oh, that. Well, you see, I was nervous then. He explained it to me. Then he thought we should have a little drink, and we did . . ."

"Only he didn't have the same drink as you did."

"Well, of course, he explained that."

"Of course. I keep forgetting that modern Arab rulers have also to be expert politicians."

"Oh, shut up, Jonas. He explained that drinks are like people, certain ones are more suitable for women, and certain ones for men. Don't you think he is right?"

"Who am I to argue with royalty? And then, when you had had your drink, the whole day began to take on a different aspect."

"Well, I realised that we had misjudged the Prince, if that is what you mean. Who can blame a man for being a little anxious about his life? For taking whatever measures he can to preserve it? But when I told him that we worked for Israeli Intelligence, and that our sole object in life was to preserve his health, he really became very friendly, and you are the proof of that, aren't you? I mean, look at you, free, and well, and in the Prince's cabin, talking to me . . ."

"Whereas he did more than talk."

Little pink spots glowed in her cheeks. "He was very kind."

"Yeah. Well, now listen very carefully. As you say, I am free and well and reasonably in control of things. But to accomplish that much I had to dispose of the main part of the Prince's crew."

"You didn't. You couldn't have."

"They were careless. And now I have to leave, for a short while, with the Prince. So you will have to hold the fort until I come back. Do you think you could manage that?"

"Why, of course I can." But she was frowning. "You say the Master is leaving the ship? Then shouldn't I come too? After all, it is part of our job to protect him."

"He is going to return in a little while, I hope. So you and he can share another drink, this evening, if all goes well. Now you get dressed and come on deck and generally keep an eye on things. I don't think you'll have any trouble, but just in case you do, here is a pistol. So far as I know it is the only one on board."

He gave her Halma's gun. She looked at it as if she had never seen a weapon before.

"A pistol? But what will I do with a pistol?"

"Make sure you are here when we get back. Now do get dressed, darling. Time is passing."

He closed the door behind him, left her sitting there staring at him. Walid was sitting at the dining table, smiling at him. "I suggested you wait," he said. "She will be, how shall I put it, my willing slave for some time yet. Certainly until the memory both of the drug and of our liaison has worn off."

Wilde watched Halma coming in from forward; she had removed her dress and instead put on a deep blue one-piece bathing costume; there was a belt round her waist with a knife in it, and she carried a pair of goggles in her right hand. She was an extraordinarily beautiful young woman.

"And just how long, do you think, will that take?" he wondered.

CHAPTER 7

The sun had set, and the mist was rolling up the valleys and shrouding the hilltops. The sea was already vanishing behind them, and the silence was intense. *Female Spirit* might have been the only ship in the world, anchored off an empty island on an empty ocean.

"Now it really is up to you two," Wilde told Jonquil and Bruno, who was looking suitably determined. "We shall be back in a couple of hours, if all goes well. But for the time being we want all the lights switched on, and some music playing, and a general amount of hustle and bustle on board, as if we were normally at anchor, and enjoying ourselves."

Jonquil was inspecting the Prince. He had put on his bathing trunks, and, now that Wilde was regarding him with a comparative eye, seemed younger and more youthful than ever. He wondered what he would look like without his beard. "I wish someone would tell me what is going on," Jonquil said.

"We are going fishing," Wilde told her. "Now, Bruno, I would like you to assist Miss Malone in every possible way. I am assuming that Madeleine is in a safe place?"

"She is in a safe place, Mr. Wilde," Halma said.

"Good. Then I'd say we could make a move. It is quite dark, and I should think the people in whom we are interested will be eating their dinner or some such thing."

"And what about *our* dinner, Mr. Wilde?" asked the Prince.

"Bruno can spend his time working on it while we're away," Wilde suggested. "Chin up, Jonquil. With any luck we'll solve this matter once and for all, tonight."

"I still think I should be coming with you," she said dreamily.

"You're not in the mood for it," Wilde reminded her. "We might just have to bop someone, fairly hard."

He followed the Prince and Halma down the accommodation ladder. Halma sat in the bow of the rubber tender, and the Prince in the stern; but Wilde did not intend to risk alerting the people on shore by using the outboard. He sat amidships with the oars, and Halma cast off. Gently he stroked the little boat away from the side of the yacht, making for the spit of land which halved the bay. Now the last of the sun had disappeared, and the night was suddenly intensely black. And despite the mist, which seemed to have come lower, it remained pleasantly warm.

"There is nothing like the Mediterranean," Walid said reflectively. "What a pity it is impossible to live here."

"I'd have thought everything was possible to the Prince of Xanda," Wilde remarked. "How are we situated for that spit, Halma?"

"Fifty metres," she said.

"Well, I aim to snuggle in on this side and either make fast to a rock or drop the hook. But it would be unfortunate if we were to puncture our skin on a sharp head. So keep a lookout, there's a dear."

She leaned over the bows. "It is difficult to see beneath the surface in the dark."

"Keep trying." He turned the bows, directing them immediately towards the spur.

"Do you know," said the Prince, "that I am quite excited? As I explained, my violence has always been at second hand. My parades have always been for show. But now I am actually going to take part in a decisive action."

"Let's hope it is decisive," Wilde said. "And for them, and not us."

There was a slight jar from beneath the dinghy.

"We have hit a rock," Halma said unnecessarily.

"Ssssh," Wilde said, and listened for the hiss of escaping air. But there was none. He shipped the oars. "Gently now," he whispered. "We do not want to make a noise."

They were still some twenty feet from the land, and he could not risk harming the boat. He thrust his legs into the milk warm sea, and lowered his body behind them. He held on to the side of the dinghy, and cautiously explored the depths with his feet. The outcrop of rock seemed to loom above his head, adding to the darkness, and now from behind them there came a blare of music. Bruno and Jonquil were obeying their instructions.

His toes encountered rock. "Pass me the grapple," he whispered, and Halma handed the small anchor over the bow. Wilde lowered it beneath him, slowly, into the water, felt it touch the rock, and jerked it free to let it go a little farther, then gave it several horizontal pulls. It caught, and settled. "Okay," he said. "She'll be here when we want her."

"You next, Halma," the Prince commanded.

The girl crawled amidships, and slowly lowered herself into the water beside Wilde. A moment later the Prince joined them.

"Breast stroke," Wilde whispered. "And try to make as little splash as possible."

Cautiously he made his way amongst the rocks; he had no wish to split open his legs on the sharp teeth. But only a few seconds' swimming brought him to the shore, and he climbed out, to crawl in the darkness until he reached a level, there to crouch until Halma and the Prince joined him. Then he led them up again, over the unevenly sloping earth, up and then down, until they had crossed the spur and gained the inner bay.

Now he could see the tent, showing white in the darkness, and illuminated by a glowing lamp within. And within too there was a woman; he could see her silhouette through the canvas. Carmel?

Beyond there was a glowing fire, and a man, sitting on the ground and cleaning a rifle.

"Long odds," the Prince whispered.

"Only if he gets to use it," Wilde said. "It's our business to see that he doesn't."

The air was at last starting to chill, just a little, for the mist seemed to have settled on the very surface of the water, and even their flesh was suddenly shrouded in drops of glistening dew, replacing the now dried salt water. But from behind them the music continued to blare, a trifle muted now by distance, but none the less evidence of a convivial evening.

But in here all was peaceful and utterly quiet. These people were waiting. For what? For whom? And where was *Esmeralda?* Gone for reinforcements?

But having come this far there was no point in returning without finishing the job, however uneasy he suddenly felt.

"Now," he whispered, "I will go first. You will come after."

He crawled over the last of the rocks, reached the sand, rose to his feet and moved forward. The man started at the sound, turned, and reached for the rifle. But Wilde was already too close. He swung the edge of his hand sideways, and struck his opponent across the head; the man fell to his hands and knees and rolled against the tent.

An explosion seemed to fill the night. Where the bullet went he had no idea, but it had passed close enough to singe him, and he instinctively dropped to his knees behind the man he had just felled. Perhaps it would be necessary to kill after all.

But it was not necessary. Carmel Wane gave a shriek of pain, and looked at Halma as if she were seeing a ghost; the Xandan girl had thrown her knife, and it had taken Carmel in the right shoulder, from whence it still protruded, through the yellow blouse which was slowly staining with red. And the pistol was dropping from her fingers to the ground.

"You are a girl of many parts, Halma," Wilde said.

"For the first time in my life," the Prince remarked, "I feel inadequate. You will either be very good for me, Mr. Wilde, or very bad. Do you know these people?"

"The lady and I are old friends. How are you, Miss Wane?"

Carmel Wane was holding her shoulder; blood seeped through her fingers. She said nothing.

"Another of these strong, silent characters," Wilde explained. "Like Madeleine."

Her breath was a long hiss.

"I will take the knife." Halma went up to the woman. "It will hurt." She seized the haft and tugged. The blade came out cleanly, but the flow of blood increased. Carmel gave a little moan and fell to her knees.

"I think you had better go back and fetch the dinghy, Halma," Wilde said. "We don't want to spend any more time here than we have to. And if you would gather up those guns, Excellency." He knelt beside the blond woman. Quickly he tore off her blouse, rolled it up into a ball to stroke away the worst of the blood, and pressed it against the wound. It was a clean cut. But it was deep. The white brassiere was also turning red now.

And still she stared at him.

"And do you know the man as well?" The Prince held Carmel's revolver in his right hand, the rifle in his left. He stood above the man, who was sitting up and holding the side of his head. He was a fairly big fellow, heavy shouldered and with powerful legs—he wore only a shirt over his bathing trunks. His face was curiously sharp, which gave his head the impression of coming together into an axe blade. It was a strong face, and an intelligent one, and it guarded a quick brain, Wilde estimated. His eyes flickered, took in the situation, and went passive. He was prepared to be patient, and by his own standards Wilde adjudged a patient man to be the most dangerous of all.

"Can't say we've met," he said. "Does he have a name, Carmel?"

Carmel Wane stared at him.

"Suffering from shock?" Wilde asked. "I tell you what, hold this shirt against your puncture, and I'll see what I can find. Do keep looking at them, Excellency."

He went into the tent. There were two sleeping bags, two rucksacks, and in the centre, a VHF transmitter. Just what he had feared. There was also, in Carmel's rucksack, a first-aid box. He had never doubted that she would be that efficient.

He returned to kneel beside the woman. "I think a spot of iodine is what you need. I'm sure Halma's knife wasn't sterilised. Do I brush it on or pour it on, Carmel? Or do you tell us about your friend?"

Carmel's mouth opened, and again she seemed to hiss at him.

"I always knew you were a brave girl," Wilde said, and uncorked the little bottle.

Carmel's nostrils dilated as the smell reached up to them. "His name is Steve, and he is not important," she said.

"I think you have to let us be the judges of that," Wilde told her. "But all in good time." He soaked a piece of cotton wool with the iodine, and as gently as he could cleansed the wound. Then he bandaged it. By now the chatter of the outboard was spreading across the night, and a few minutes later Halma and the dinghy appeared out of the mist, sliding into the shallows.

"You'll have to get your feet wet," Wilde said. He made Carmel and the man called Steve sit amidships, on the rubber deck of the dinghy. The Prince sat forward, holding the weapons. Halma sat aft next to Wilde; her shoulder brushed his as he controlled the outboard and steered out of the bay. Water lapped over the gunwale, but a few moments later the lights of *Female Spirit* came into sight; the music was still blaring into the night.

Wilde brought the dinghy up to the accommodation ladder, checked it with a short burst astern.

"Mr. Wilde," the Prince said. "Allow me to congratulate you. A masterly operation. Cutting them out, you said. I must remember that. Cutting them out."

"I think we should get them safely on board, Excellency," Wilde suggested.

"Up," the Prince commanded, and stuck the gun muzzle into Steve's back. "You had better help your wounded friend."

Steve helped Carmel on to the ladder, and she went up very slowly, the man at her elbow.

"Keep the gun on them, Jonquil," Wilde called up. "And you can turn off that beastly row."

The Prince was now on the ladder as well, and Wilde held the foot of the steps to steady it. Carmel reached the deck, and was followed by Steve.

"Believe me," the Prince said as he gained the gangway. "To watch this man Wilde at work is a remarkable business. He accomplishes things which you or I would regard as difficult or even impossible without the slightest hesitation. I suppose it is all confidence, in his ability, in his past successes. I envy you, Jonquil. Jonquil?"

The note in his voice made Wilde look up, and instinctively move on to the ladder. From above him there came a gasp.

"I have wanted to do that for years," Madeleine said. "We have the Prince, Wilde. If you do not surrender we shall kill him, now."

ii

Before Wilde could come to a decision there was another gasp, and a shout from above him. He clung to the ladder as it shook, and looked up in horror as the Prince's body came arching back off the gangway, while Madeleine shouted and a gun went off. Walid spun through the air, desperately kicking in an attempt to regain his balance and straighten himself out, and then struck the tender with a huge whumpff; the weapons he had carried spun away into the night.

"Master," Halma shouted as she fell overboard at the stern.

Now the shooting commenced in earnest from above, and someone was calling for the use of the searchlight. Wilde slithered back down the ladder and fell beside the Prince, just at the moment a bullet tore into the rubber hull, and the dinghy exploded with a gigantic hiss; he lost touch with the Prince, as he went deep into the water, but regained the surface a moment later, and homed in on the splashes close to him. Now there was pandemonium from the big ship, voices shouting, and now too the searchlight was starting to play on the sea.

"I have been hit," the Prince panted. "I have been hit, Mr. Wilde."

"Where?"

"I think it is in the leg. It is very painful."

"Halma? Where are you, Halma?"

"I am here, Mr. Wilde." She trod water at his elbow.

"We have got to get the hell out of here," he said.

"But the Master is wounded. He must have help."

"We'll not find much around here. Let's get him ashore. One each side. Over there."

Immediately in front of them, parallel with the ship, the cliffs rose dark and sombre even against the backdrop of the night.

"You fool," Carmel was sobbing. "You should just have shot him. Oh, you fool, Madeleine."

"We'll get them," Madeleine promised. "There's no place for them to go. Get down," she bawled. "Get the other dinghy into the water. They can't be far."

"Come on," Wilde said. "Quietly now."

He turned on his back, stroked with his feet, holding Walid's shoulders. Halma swam on the other side. The Prince sighed, and his head suddenly drooped. Wilde jerked it up again.

"Let's have some princely resolution, Excellency," he said. "If you can just keep awake until we reach land, you will be all right."

Now they were perhaps fifty feet away from the yacht, and they could see two men, already ghostlike in the mist, lowering the other rubber dinghy, peering into the water beside it. Two men. One was no doubt the man Carmel called Steve. Who the other one could be, what had happened on board, what part Jonquil Malone had played in the disaster . . . imagination boggled. Jonquil Malone.

"May Allah have mercy on my soul," Walid whispered. "I am going to die."

"You cannot die, Master," Halma said.

"It would be both inconvenient and a waste of my time," Wilde pointed out. "Just keep counting oil wells, Excellency. It's not far now."

But it was farther than he had estimated, and now someone called up from the dinghy. "There is no one around here. Shine the light farther off. They must be trying for the shore."

"Take a deep breath," Wilde said. "We are going to have to submerge."

The Prince sighed. Wilde watched the beam of light sweeping to and fro as it left the side of the yacht and slowly covered the open water.

"Now," he said, and sucked himself under, taking the Prince with him. Legs kicked, and he looked up to see the light immediately above them. Then legs kicked again, and the Prince slithered away.

Wilde cursed silently, kicked down himself, and burst into the light. There were shouts of excitement, and of triumph, from the yacht. "There's a problem," he gasped. "Come on, Halma." He grasped one of the Prince's armpits with his left hand, urged his right and his feet to stroke as fast as he could. Halma followed his example on the far side.

"I could not breathe," the Prince groaned. "I could not breathe. The pain . . ."

"Mr. Wilde," Halma said urgently. "Mr. Wilde."

He twisted on to his belly, gazed at the rocks, rising above him, jagged where they were not sheer. There was no suggestion of a beach, no suggestion even of a ledge where they could rest. As if they could possibly rest, unarmed and with a crippled man. And still the searchlight rested on them, and behind them an outboard chattered into life.

"We are all going to die," the Prince groaned. "I thank you, my friends, for the efforts you have made on my behalf. But I shall only be able to reward you in heaven."

"You talk too bloody much," Wilde said. He was beginning to feel a little despairing himself. But that was because he was exhausted; rivers of pain were running up and down his muscles. It had been one of the longest days of his life, had contained as much violent action as he had ever known in a span of twenty-four hours, and there was no question of its ending yet.

The searchlight was beginning to fade as it diffused in the mist, but now the rubber dinghy was approaching, and a glance over his shoulder showed him one man in the stern, controlling the outboard, and the other kneeling in the bow. This one held a pistol. Jonquil's pistol. At least he could thank God the Prince had allowed no rifles on board. He was tempted to turn back and try to upset them, but he was afraid that to release the Prince would be to lose him.

They were now close enough to see the sheer rock face in front of them, an endless expanse of red wall, sheer and unpromising, except where there was a sudden darker shadow closed by the water's edge.

A sudden shadow. "Over there," he gasped. "Make haste."

He forgot about the splashes, kicked vigorously and made for the darkness. Halma swam as fast on the other side of the Prince, yet it seemed an eternity before they reached the shadow, and were swept into it by the next gentle surge. For as he had suspected, it was the arc of a cave. The men in the dinghy shouted, and the outboard went into neutral as the man in the bow opened fire. But he was firing blind, and the bullets merely crunched into the rocks.

But now Wilde heard a new and entirely unwelcome sound; the growl of twin diesels. These he recognised. *Esmeralda* had not been very far off, as he had suspected, and was coming to the rescue. But not of the Prince.

"I cannot see," Halma said.

"That's half the battle," Wilde said, treading water and peering into the almost solid darkness. Now it was suddenly airless and close, and they could not even see the sides of the cavern in which they swam. Nor the roof, nor the water beneath them. An impenetrable darkness, in which there might be lurking untold hideous monsters. What nonsense. But how basic is man's fear of the dark and the unknown, he thought.

"The Prince has fainted, Mr. Wilde," Halma said.

Just the help they needed. Wilde uttered a silent prayer, struck to his left, and encountered rock. The cave was even narrower than he had supposed; they must have been swimming in the exact centre, surely. He fumbled at the rock, and discovered that there was a ledge. How wide, he wondered, desperately holding the Prince's head above water, because, as Halma had said, Walid was unconscious, and his nose kept dipping forward.

"He *will* die, Mr. Wilde," Halma whispered. "If we do not get him out of the water."

"So let's try what we have here," Wilde said. "Can you support him for a moment?"

"I think so," she said.

Wilde released the shoulder he had been holding, and turned to the ledge. He thrust an arm over, explored the rock. It seemed to be at least two feet wide, which was better than he could have hoped. He got both his elbows over, kicked down, and lodged a knee, then got his whole body up.

"Now, then," he said. "Can you give him a push from underneath as I drag him up?"

"I will try," she agreed.

Wilde locked his fingers in the Prince's armpits, braced his body as best he could, counted to three, and lifted. Halma gave a little squeak as she pushed and went under the surface. For a moment the Prince hung, held only by Wilde's fingers. It was necessary to give another great heave and gasp to hook him on to the ledge itself.

Cautiously Wilde explored himself for any suggestion of hernia, then he laid the Prince out flat, and once more turned to the water. "Are you still with us?"

"I think so, Mr. Wilde."

"Give me your hands."

He swept the darkness, encountering a head of wet hair, and felt her fingers close on his wrists. Another heave, and she fell over him on to the ledge itself. For a moment they lay against each other, panting, while water drained out of their hair and their swim suits and down their legs.

"I had not realised how tired I was," she whispered.

"Well, brace yourself, because I suspect we're still an hour or two from bed. First thing, the Prince." He squeezed past her, found the unconscious man's legs, explored the flesh. The right leg seemed to be all right; the wound was in the second one, above the knee, so far as he could tell; he could feel the serrated edge of bone just under the surface of the skin, and the skin itself was torn. His fingers were immediately wet, but there seemed to be surprisingly little blood. Nor could he discover any trace of the bullet.

"Christ Almighty," he muttered.

"It is bad, Mr. Wilde?"

"You don't believe in exaggeration, I'm glad to see. You could say, it is bad."

"And we cannot see it," she said.

"Never state the obvious. It's always bad news. But we have to bind it up, or he will die from loss of blood. Do you mind going topless for a while?"

"Not if it will help the Prince." She handed him the sodden scrap of cloth, and he suddenly remembered that she hadn't, after all, been wearing a bikini. "It is not much."

"More than I expected," Wilde said. "It'll certainly stop the bleeding. All we have to do is keep him quiet until we can get some help in here."

Help, is what we need, he thought; as he tied the bathing suit around the wound, he heard the sound of the outboard approaching.

CHAPTER 8

"Lie flat," Wilde snapped, and did so himself, trying to make his body seem part of the ledge. And just in time, because a moment later the beam of a torch swept the cavern, to and fro, slowly, confidently. And the outboard stopped chattering. But he could not see beyond the light.

"Wilde," Madeleine called. "We know you are in there, Wilde. I suggest you show yourself and surrender."

Wilde pressed himself to the rock. He could feel Halma's breath on his toes, and prayed that she would keep down. And that the Prince would not wake up.

"Listen to me, Wilde," Madeleine said. "I am offering you your life. We only wish to destroy the Prince. If you come out, with the girl, we shall let you go. Did you seriously suppose you were the only trump in our hand? Oh no, Wilde. You were only the thin edge of the wedge, to put the Prince off his guard. How were we to know that you would destroy his crew, and make life so easy for us. Come out, Wilde, and I'll even kiss you."

There was a short silence. Wilde felt Halma's hand on his leg, and reached down to squeeze it. Her own grip was reassuring.

Madeleine spoke again. "Listen to me, Wilde. We have dynamite here, enough to blow in this entrance. There is no one for miles, to hear the bang. But you will be trapped in there, Wilde. There is no way out of that cave. We know the Prince is hurt. The odds are that he will die very rapidly in any event, without help. Why sacrifice yourself as well? Think about that, Wilde. We will give you thirty seconds."

"Mr. Wilde," Halma whispered.

"Sssh," Wilde said.

"But it will mean your death."

"And yours, Halma."

"It is my duty to die with my master."

"Well, it is my duty to keep him alive as long as I can. Stay flat. Anyway, don't you think they'll do us all the moment we go out?"

"Time is up, Wilde," Madeleine called. "Are the charges placed, Steve?"

"They're placed," the man said.

"Very well. Pull us back, Clem."

The other man worked the outboard, and the light withdrew. Now who the hell is Clem? Wilde wondered.

"We could make a dash for it," Halma suggested.

"We'd get blown up and shot up all at once. And what would we do with his nibs? We can only sit this one out. Keep your head down."

Almost as he spoke there was a tremendous rush of air, which seemed to come at him like a solid force, and hit him some seconds before the noise. But that too was almost physical, reverberating around him, crashing on his eardrums, and was followed by a succession of other noise waves, while the water in the cavern, a few minutes before more than a foot below the level of the ledge, suddenly slapped him on the face and slurped over his arm.

He thought perhaps he lost consciousness for a few seconds. Then he was aware that the noise was receding, although there was still a continuous rumble of sound from the entrance. But even that soon faded, and the cavern was still; it was possible to hear the high-pitched plop of a drop of water from the roof.

"Mr. Wilde?" Halma's whisper ghosted at him.

"Still here, sweetheart." He pushed down with his hands, sat up, and leaned against the wall, dangling his feet over the edge. "Where are you?"

Her fingers touched his shoulder. "Are we going to die, Mr. Wilde?"

"Not immediately. The air isn't all that bad. Our first job must be to find somewhere safe for the Prince to lie; this ledge is a trifle narrow. Let me pass."

He got back on to his hands and knees, crawled against her. She flattened herself next to the inside wall and he wriggled by.

"Where are you going, Mr. Wilde?"

"I'm going to trace this ledge for a while. It may broaden out, or it may come to a full stop."

"You will be careful, Mr. Wilde? Please. I should not like to be left here, alone in the darkness."

Wilde smiled at where he supposed her to be. "I'll be careful, Halma."

He moved very slowly, placing one hand well in front of the place he next hoped to place his knee, and keeping his balance well back so as not to fall into any unsuspected holes. And before every forward movement he tested the rock face on his left, and the void to his right. But for several minutes nothing changed. At the end of that time he sat down, both to rest, because it was surprisingly tiring, and to dangle his feet over the side. But once again his toes touched water.

Now he waited, listening to the silence, to the occasional plop of water. Not a sufficiently continuous plop to suggest stalactites. But still, no foul air. That was his main worry.

He resumed his journey, hand in front of hand, knee in front of knee. He crawled, for what seemed several hours, but could only have been a few minutes. And then his left hand pushed out to touch the wall, encountered only space. He was so surprised he nearly fell over, but he caught himself in time, swept his hand round and round in the darkness. There was definitely no wall. But the ledge continued in front of him, although obviously it had widened.

Here was a problem. Supposing he had entered a larger cave? To follow the left-hand wall right round, which was the safest thing to do in this darkness, might take several hours. And then, it might be a side tunnel. But to go straight across would be to lose touch with his only means of perspective. Once he stepped out into this Stygian blackness he could never hope to tell right from left, up from down, again.

But certainly this piece of rock was wide enough for a man to lie upon, and even roll a little, without necessarily falling back into the water. It was their best bet so far.

Carefully he turned round, and made his way back along the ledge. "Halma?"

"Yes, Mr. Wilde." Her voice came from farther away than he had supposed. He must have been crawling for longer than he had thought, as well.

"Just making sure where you are." He went towards her.

"Have you found something, Mr. Wilde?"

"A safer place for his nibs. Any sign of life?"

"No, Mr. Wilde. But he is breathing evenly."

"That's a good thing. Although we don't want to wake him up if we can help it. I'll take his shoulders, and we'll pull him along."

"That will bruise the Master's back, Mr. Wilde."

"Can't be helped. I'll be as gentle as I can. You get down his other end, and try to keep that leg from banging about. Think you can manage that?"

"Yes, Mr. Wilde."

She crawled away from him. Wilde knelt, got his hands into the Prince's armpits once again, and began to retreat along the ledge. This was considerably more difficult than going forward, and he had no real sense of position. All he could do was keep his right shoulder pressed against the rock face as he went backwards. But soon he was exhausted, and sweat poured out of his hair and down his back to meet the pain rising from his tired muscles.

And now the Prince groaned, and stirred. "Halma?" he muttered. "Halma? What is happening to me, Halma?"

"You are in a cavern, Master, with Mr. Wilde and me. We are moving you to a place of safety, Master. You are wounded."

"My leg. By Allah, I remember, my leg. Allah, how it hurts. Mr. Wilde? Why are we still in this cave?"

"Mainly because I haven't found a way out yet, Excellency," Wilde explained. "They blew in the front."

"Ah, yes," the Prince said. "I thought I had dreamed that. It seems that we are shut in here forever, Mr. Wilde."

"Forever is one of those words we don't use in my business, Excellency. It has all sorts of nasty undertones. Now if you can grit your teeth for a few minutes more, we'll have you off this ledge and on to a sort of platform. I can't be sure because I can't see."

"I will bear it, Mr. Wilde," the Prince said. "You may recommence."

"Aye, aye," Wilde said, and resumed dragging the body along the rock. He could hear the Prince breathing now, the air rasping through the tortured nostrils, while the flesh in his hands, which had been almost dry and certainly cool to the touch, became hot and clammy with sweat. But apparently the Prince could take it as well as dish it out. And at last, behind him, the rock was opening out.

"Here we are," he said. "Now, I don't know what we are on, or how large it is, or what lies beyond. So under no circumstances must we lose contact with each other. Preferably we should stay within touching distance. Understood?"

"I understand, Mr. Wilde." Walid sighed. "I am in agony. I do not think I am going to be able to bear the pain very much longer. I should not like to cry out, Mr. Wilde."

"It would probably set up an echo," Wilde agreed.

"So I would take it as a favour, Mr. Wilde, if you would hit me and knock me unconscious. I imagine a man like yourself could render me unconscious with a single blow. Is that not so?"

"It's probable. If I could see just where I was hitting you in the dark, Excellency. But I am not sure it is the right solution. You are unlikely to remain unconscious very long, from a punch on the jaw, and when you woke up you would just have another set of pains to brood on."

"May I help you, Master?" Halma asked.

"By Allah," the Prince said. "I had forgotten the girl."

"I am always here, Master," Halma said. "It was your command that I always be here."

"Yes, child. Yes. You may help me, Halma." The Prince sighed. It occurred to Wilde that he could probably find something for her to do which would take his mind off his immediate problems. And soon there was a great deal of heavy breathing from close by. Which wasn't so good, from the point of view of an overtired and somewhat chilled man sitting alone in the darkness wearing only a pair of bathing trunks.

He crawled back along the ledge, sat down, his legs dangling in the water. Now the sounds were muted. And he could think. If he could summon the energy, and the morale. There was a strong argument for having a sleep, to awake refreshed. The air remained fresh enough. That didn't mean a thing, as regards getting out; it might be filtering in by any number of little channels through the rocks above, but it certainly suggested they were in no danger of dying of suffocation.

On the other hand, Carmel Wane and her friends would be well aware that they might not be dying of suffocation.

But they would be putting some faith in the Prince's wound. There was the real problem. He had to be got to hospital, and as quickly as possible.

So then, what about the explosion in the cave mouth? It had apparently blocked it up, but he could not be sure of that in the dark. There was every possibility of the blockage not being complete, especially under water. Unfortunately, even if he found a channel through, there was no possibility of taking the Prince out that way. And here again, it would be wishful thinking to suppose that Carmel Wane had not thought of that one as well. She would be prepared to wait. Tomorrow, and the day after. And for the next week, if she chose. There was no law to prevent a yacht like *Female Spirit* from dropping anchor in a pleasantly secluded Corsican bay and staying there for the rest of the summer. Nor was there any law to keep them from coming ashore, from having someone, just for instance, sitting on the cliff top, bird watching, all day and all night. Just in case there *was* an exit.

Their only risk would be bad weather from the west, which would force them to put to sea; this particular cove would be untenable in a strong westerly.

But even that would not necessarily scotch their plans. They could always leave a watchdog ashore for the day or two the blow would be likely to last, and a big sea running outside would effectively prevent Wilde from escaping by the cave mouth, even if he could find the way through.

But it had to be done, if it were possible, and as soon as possible. Every moment he remained here reduced Walid's chances and increased Carmel's.

Okay, so supposing he got out. What then? This was the most deserted part of Corsica. The nearest telephone was probably fifty miles away.

If only he could tell what had happened, and was now happening, on board the yacht. How in the name of God had Madeleine got free and upset the apple cart? That could only have been with the assistance of Jonquil Malone. She had been left in charge. How she must have smiled, as the rubber dinghy had paddled away into the night. How she must have smiled from the beginning, at Wilde's frantic gyrations.

Christ Almighty, he thought. If you, Jonas Wilde, ever trust a woman again, any woman, any sort of woman, you should be locked up in a home for backward children.

There was a slither beside him. "Are you there, Mr. Wilde?" Halma whispered.

"Oh, aye. Counting sheep."

"Sheep, Mr. Wilde? There can be no sheep in this cave."

"Unfortunately, you are absolutely right. Which makes the whole operation rather futile. How is the chief?"

"He is sleeping, Mr. Wilde. I soothed him to sleep."

"I wonder how you accomplished that?" Wilde asked. "Seeing as how he was in agony."

"The Prince is often in agony, Mr. Wilde," she explained. "He suffers from neuralgia, and sometimes cannot sleep at all, for the pain. And he will not take drugs, because he thinks it is debilitating for a human being to drug himself, and also because he can never tell whether or not the drugs may have been tampered with. When he suffers like that, Mr. Wilde, not even women can satisfy him. Ordinary women."

"But you are no ordinary woman."

"I have been specially trained, yes, Mr. Wilde. But now I would ask you what you wish me to do."

"I'm not sure I can think of anything useful, at the moment."

"Well, then, Mr. Wilde, would you make love to me?"

ii

It occurred to Wilde that that was actually something he wanted to do, very badly, and in this position it would be best not to have more on his mind than was absolutely necessary.

Nor did it seem to occur to Halma for a second that he might possibly refuse her.

"It would be better," she said, "if we went back to the broad ledge."

"I'm sure you're right." He put out his hand, but could not find her. So he crawled, cautiously. He did not wish to wake up the Prince again. And then he discovered the girl. Or she discovered him; he could not be sure. She was still warm from her previous exertions, and as she had promised, she had been specially trained, with just one object in mind. Correction, he remembered; two objects. She was as useful with a pistol or a knife as with everything else. But there was a great deal else.

"Mr. Wilde," she whispered, her lips on his ear, "Mr. Wilde, you are a *man*. I knew that, when first we met."

"And you have been reserved exclusively to the Prince."

"He also is a man," she said. "But not so . . ." She hesitated.

"Not so anxious to share, maybe," Wilde said. "Tell me how you came to belong to him."

Her body moved against his as she shrugged. "I have been his for several years. Every year, in Xanda, there is a selection of girls for the Prince. Only the best half-dozen ever get to see him personally. Most of the rest are weeded out by the vizier. But there are always six. They will be about thirteen years of age, and must just have attained puberty."

"He took you at that age?"

"Not to his bed, Mr. Wilde. But I was taken into the harem, and sent to school there, to learn to read and write and sing and speak, pleasingly to the Prince, and to learn the ways of men with women, and the ways men wish of women."

"But for you there was an additional lesson."

"For me, yes," she said. "For many reasons, I think. Because I am not pure Xandan. My father was a Frenchman who owned a cafe. This gave me an additional height, and a different colouring from the other girls, and so I interested the Prince more. He found me pleasing. And then he found that my eyesight was unusually good, my reactions unusually quick. He told me, once, smiling, that my father must have been a remarkable man, because there was nothing remarkable about my mother. And then he decided that he would have me with him, always. So I was sent back to school. To a different school, Mr. Wilde, where I was taught to shoot and to use a knife, and how to hurt a man, or a woman, with my hands alone."

"I've been to that school too," Wilde said.

"That I know. And then I was made a bodyguard to the Prince. For four years I was his sole bodyguard, until the woman Madeleine."

There was jealousy in her voice now, and anger, and even hate. She was no brainwashed automaton.

"But you never suspected that Madeleine might be a plant?"

"It is not my place to suspect things, Mr. Wilde. She was placed over me, and I was obliged to take her orders. That is all I had to understand. She replaced me also in the Prince's bed. This too I had to understand."

"And you resented this."

For a moment she did not reply. "I resented it, Mr. Wilde. But I think I was more frightened. It is not permitted for a woman who has known the Prince to know other men, to do other things. She must be shut away, with her fellows. For most girls that does not happen until they are no longer pleasing to the Prince, but for me, in my special position, I did not know what would become of me."

"But you were not immediately retired."

"No, Mr. Wilde."

"Because Madeleine figured you might just be useful one day, I imagine. But now, Halma, what happens next? You have committed the sin of sins. Or have you sinned before?"

"No, Mr. Wilde, I have never sinned before. There has never been any reason. For me, the Prince has filled the entire world. There was no man like the Prince. I thought, in my innocence, that there could never be any man like the Prince. But when I was told to arrest you, and you disposed of me so easily, and when, later, I saw you destroy the entire ship's company, so easily . . ."

"I'm beginning to wonder if I did the right thing," Wilde admitted. "Not on your account, Halma. In view of the present situation."

"You did the right thing, Mr. Wilde, for me. You made me see that there are other men in the world besides the Prince. You made me realise how limited had been my horizons. You made me realise that the Prince was, after all, no more than a man. I knew, then, that I had to possess your body, and that you had to possess mine. Even if the Prince had me executed for it, that had to happen."

"Well, don't worry about it. I have never been one to kiss and tell."

"But *I* must tell him, Mr. Wilde. I swore an oath, on the Koran, to be faithful to him and none other. I have broken that oath. I could not have broken it, had I not known that all three of us must die, here in this cavern. But as we are, why, it does not matter. Yet I cannot go to my grave with such a sin on my conscience. So I must confess to him, and tell him, too, that he has been outmatched in the most essential of man's functions. For what is violence? A man may murder a hundred people with a bomb or a machine gun. But a man may only satisfy one woman at a time, properly. And you have satisfied me beyond my wildest dreams. Now I will die happy, Mr. Wilde."

"I'm sure you shall," Wilde said. "Let's hope that goes for all of us. But now, if you don't mind, I think I'll see if I can find a way out of this hole. It'll be so crowded when we all wake up, don't you think?"

iii

Halma's hands slid over his back and up to his shoulders. "You said we should not lose contact, Mr. Wilde. If you swim away into the darkness, how will we find each other?"

"I think I'll be able to. Find you, I mean. I'm just going to have a look at the rock fall. Any time you feel lonely, sing out. And when I want to come back, all I have to do is follow the ledge. Right?"

Her hands still rested on his shoulders, and now her mouth drifted across his cheek. "I will be here, Mr. Wilde. I will be here, always. I promise you that, Mr. Wilde. As of this moment, I will always be at your side."

"Even after telling His Excellency how you've let him down? I would say that is probably a capital offence."

"It is, Mr. Wilde. It is an insult to the princely power. But for it to be efficacious, the punishment, I mean, both the guilty parties must be executed, in secrecy. No word of what has happened must ever get out. So the Prince will never be able to execute me, Mr. Wilde, as he will not be able to execute you."

"I wish I could come round to your point of view. It all seems so simple."

"It is simple, Mr. Wilde. How can the Prince, or anyone, execute a man of so many talents."

"In Xanda they would probably tie me to a stake and put a rope around my neck, and then slip a stick through the rope and give it a few twists."

"And would you not break the rope, Mr. Wilde?"

"I might try."

"And in any event, Mr. Wilde, the Prince would never harm you, because he respects you. I have never heard, I have never seen, such respect, in the Prince for any man. He will never harm you, Mr. Wilde. And so he will never harm the woman you love."

Wilde scratched his head. He thought it would be safer not to comment.

"So I will tell him what happened," Halma said. "And I will ask him to give me to you. Will that not solve everything, Mr. Wilde?"

"Not everything," Wilde said. "It is surprising how there are always a few loose ends lying around, no matter how things are tied up."

"I am not worried about loose ends, Mr. Wilde. I am sure everything is going to turn out all right. I am happy, now. I do not remember ever having been happy before. I am not going to be unhappy, again, ever."

"That's my girl. But it's going to be a short celebration if we don't get out of here. So you just sit tight, and let me nose around for a while."

He slipped away into the darkness before she could say anything more, made his way along the ledge, reached the end and lowered himself into the water, swam close to the sheer rock wall beyond, more carefully than before, thrusting his hands in front of himself. It was as uncomfortably eerie now as it had been when coming in. Even more so, perhaps. If there had been any unpleasant creatures lurking in the cave, they would certainly have been disturbed by the bang. And that went even for moray eels.

He touched broken rock, stopped swimming. Slowly he pulled himself along, trying to estimate distance as best he could. He remembered the entrance as being perhaps eight feet across. Now it occurred to him that the rock fall was wider than that. Say ten feet. It had been a powerful explosive. But then, the force of the blast had suggested that.

And there was no suggestion of air coming in from the bay outside.

He took a long breath, and went down into the utter darkness. And to his surprise encountered bottom before he expected. Eight feet below the surface, he estimated. He kicked, and drove himself against the entrance. Tumbled rock lay everywhere, piled on top of the other, blocking the gap as completely as if an army of masons had been at work all evening. And now it was necessary for him to breathe again.

He kicked down, and rose, felt his head break the surface, and gulped air into his lungs. How fresh and good it tasted, on a sudden.

How fresh? He put out his hand, and found nothing. He swung his body round, reached in the other direction, and again encountered nothing but space.

"Christ Almighty," he muttered, and swam for some feet in what he thought was a seaward direction, and then stopped to tread water. Now he was quite chilled, but the cold of the water was nothing compared with the icy fingers which were darting up his neck and trying to seize his brain.

Yet he could not be far from where he had gone down; the air was once again a little heavy with the stench of mouldering rock.

Once again. But just now it had been free air, playing on his face. Christ Almighty. How to find it again. How to find anything again.

"Halma?" he shouted. The echo drifted along the darkness. "Halma?"

"Mr. Wilde?" She seemed a long way away.

"Keep shouting," Wilde bellowed.

"Mr. Wilde? Mr. Wilde? Mr. Wilde?"

He swam towards the reverberating sound. She had a high, clear voice which acted like a radio beacon. He swam as cautiously as before, pushing his hands in front of himself to avoid doing himself any permanent injury on a sudden outcrop, but found nothing, until his fingers touched a bare rock face, and immediately beyond it the ledge. And now Halma's call was very close.

"Okay," he panted. "Okay." He pulled himself out.

"Mr. Wilde?" asked the Prince. "What is happening, Mr. Wilde?"

"Sorry about that," Wilde said. "I didn't mean to wake you up, Excellency." He crawled along the ledge, encountered the cool flesh of the girl. "I got myself lost. How do you feel?"

"I am in pain, Mr. Wilde. What time is it?"

Wilde looked at his watch. "Two o'clock in the morning, Excellency."

"I was under the impression that you were going to wait until morning to seek a way out."

"I got impatient. But I think I have discovered something useful, supposing I can find it again. There's a current of fresh air coming in somewhere by the entrance. It may well be just a crack in the rock, but it may also be wide enough for a man."

"And you will try to climb up? It may lead to the summit; that is more than two hundred feet."

"Which is why I don't think it is a practical proposition for anyone save me," Wilde said. "Which involves leaving you here, Excellency."

"I will wait for you to come back with help, Mr. Wilde. Halma will keep me company, and take care of me. Will you not, child?"

There was a moment's hesitation. "Yes, Master," Halma said.

"What bothers me is that I may not come back," Wilde said. "There is no one living around here. I know this coast. It would take me a couple of days to get across the mountains to Ajaccio, if I ever made it, and I'm not sure you will last that long; you are losing blood all the time."

"Then what are you suggesting, Mr. Wilde?"

"There is a radio telephone on board *Female Spirit*. In five seconds I can have all of Corsica homing on this bay."

"Ah," the Prince said. "But so far as we know, our enemies are in possession of the ship. Would it not be safer to work your way round to the encampment, and use the radio there?"

"Unfortunately, that was a VHF set. Very high frequency, you know? Its effective range isn't much over twenty miles, and surrounded by these mountains probably somewhat less. I think they were using it merely to keep in touch with *Esmeralda*."

"So you will have to fight your way to the yacht's radio. Unarmed." The Prince smiled into the darkness. "Of course, with no weapons to speak of you destroyed my ship's company. But they had no knowledge of how dangerous you really are. Neither did I, or I would have had you shot out of hand. I am very glad I did not do so, of course, but will not that blond woman, and most certainly Madeleine, wish to kill you immediately?"

"That is what I have been suggesting, Excellency."

"And you will risk this, for me?"

"It really is a part of the job, Excellency. This isn't an assignment I'd have taken on, if I'd known just what was involved. But as I seem to have got lumbered with it, I intend to do the best I can. What I am trying to say is this; if I am going to have to take on that crowd I am going to need all the help I can get, animate and inanimate. It may involve the loss of your ship."

"*Female Spirit?* Ah." There was a moment's silence. "I begin to suspect what you have in mind, Mr. Wilde. Very well. I do not think she can be a lucky ship. And I wonder if Mediterranean cruising is really for me. Except perhaps with you as crew. By Allah, Mr. Wilde. If you will work for me when this is done, I will pay you any salary you care to name, and give you the pick of every woman in the country."

"There's a dangerous subject," Wilde said. "But you did mention the crew. I don't know what has happened to them. If they are still alive and on board, I will try to get them off. But I can't promise anything."

"You do not have to promise anything, Mr. Wilde. I have confidence in you. Should any of my men have to die, they knew the risk they were taking when they entered my service."

"I thought they might," Wilde agreed. "I'll say so long. Or whatever it is in Xandan."

"Just now you spoke of the help you would need, Mr. Wilde," Halma said. "Should I not accompany you?"

"I'll take your knife," Wilde said. "But I think your duty lies here with the Prince. Believe me, I don't think numbers are going to be quite as important as one or two other factors in this caper. Got the knife?"

He put his hand into the darkness, and a moment later hers touched it, with the haft of the knife thrust forward. Wilde squeezed her fingers, then tucked the knife into the belt of his swim suit, exactly in the centre of his back, where it could do no unintended harm.

"Have fun. And stay sober."

"Good luck, Mr. Wilde," the Prince of Xanda said.

"Good luck, Mr. Wilde," Halma said.

iv

He followed the ledge to the end, as before, then swam across to the rock fall, made his way along it to the farther side, and paddled around for a moment. But there was no draught of air. It would be necessary to repeat the entire manoeuvre all over again, and even then he was taking long odds against coming up in exactly the same place. On the other hand, he remembered that the air on his face had come down strongly, suggesting that there had been a lot of it getting in.

He sank into the water, down and down and down, touched the bottom, moved against the rock face, and kicked away again. He broke surface, tossed water from his eyes and hair, turned his face up, and felt nothing. He put out his hand, and touched wall.

"God damn and blast," he muttered. He could not have travelled far enough. Or had he only dreamed the whole thing earlier?

He swam a few feet to his right, went down, touched bottom and kicked again, and came up into the freshness he sought. He swept his hand round, and found nothing. But the air came from directly above him. How far?

He turned on his back, stared at the darkness, and saw nothing. It could have been a thousand miles to the nearest rock. Yet, strong as it was, the fresh air was coming down in a narrow stream, smaller even than an open window. That meant the roof had to be very low.

He took a long breath, tensed his muscles, stretched his arms above his head, and kicked himself upwards. And slapped rock so hard he thought he had broken a finger. He fell back into the water with a gigantic splash.

"Mr. Wilde?" Halma called. "Are you all right, Mr. Wilde?"

"Just testing."

This time he was more careful in his jump; the roof of the cave on this side was actually only about four feet above the surface; it had appeared higher in the brief light of Madeleine's torch because of the shadow.

It took four jumps to locate the actual shaft, and by then his breath was gasping and his muscles were turning to lead. And if the shaft definitely had a lip, it was still smooth rock. And he still had no idea how wide it was. The whole thing was very much like trying to land a quoit while blindfolded. But on the seventh jump he got his fingers over the edge, and hung there, panting, feeling the purchase slowly slipping away.

That would never do. He kicked down again, threw his body forward, and waited for his head to smash into something solid. Amazingly it did not, and a moment later he got his elbows over. Still they slipped, and he had to summon another immense effort to get his body into the aperture, twist sideways and lodge it there, and then almost collapse in total exhaustion, while the salt water drained from his legs and fell with steady plops into the cavern beneath.

That apart, there was no sound, save for the soughing of the wind. The wind. It came whining down the crevice, playing over him, warmer than he had expected, now he was actually in it. Certainly warmer than anything in the cave itself.

He pushed himself up, touched rock with his back. The crevice led away at roughly a forty-five-degree angle, upwards, and was, he estimated, about four feet across. Here. He could only hope that it wasn't as smooth as this all the way up.

He climbed. On his hands and knees for a while, slipping back six inches for every foot he advanced. Now his body was dry, for a second, before the sweat started to pour from his arms and his shoulders, making climbing yet more difficult. He paused to rest, and then tried turning on his back and pushing himself upwards with his feet on the far wall. This was actually a little easier on the muscles, and he made more regular progress, but it was hard on his back. And insensibly the crevice was narrowing.

But also getting rougher. He was way above any water levels now. He turned on to his belly, and began to worm his way up. He looked at his watch. It was half-past three. He had forgotten to note when he had entered the cut, but it must have been about an hour ago. And how high had he climbed in that time? A hundred feet?

He was an optimist.

He climbed, slowly, worming his way upwards, feeling the rock cutting at his chest and belly and thighs. And then his shoulders also touched.

"Oh, Christ," he muttered. To have come so far, and then to be stopped. He thrust his right hand above him, found the cliff face which was pressing in on him, swept the hand forward again, and found nothing. Pass this narrow space, and he was clear again. Until the next narrow space. He was surprised at how reluctant he was to move. Because suppose the next narrow space was only a foot or two farther up, and he could not obtain the leverage either to go on or come back?

The sudden claustrophobia made him feel physically sick, and for some seconds he could do no more than cling to his position.

But go on he must. To return was in any event to condemn all three of them to death.

He took several long breaths, and attempted to think his way through the barrier, beyond, to where the air and the light would be, and Carmel Wane. And Jonquil Malone. And Madeleine, and Steve. And anybody else who might happen to get into his way.

Slowly the anger began to build up again, to drive out the lurking fear. He dug his fingers into the rock and moved up, pressing his belly as flat as he could. Now the other wall scraped at his back, and the sharpness of the pain told him that his flesh was broken. What had the Prince told Madeleine about sharks? Because the water out there was certainly open enough.

But immediately he was distracted by a new problem. There was a flick of steel against his leg, and then a tinkle as the knife slipped out from his trunks and clattered on to the rock. And then clattered again and again as it slid away into the depths. Going back was out of the question. Ah, well, if this business ended up with a knife being the answer, he was lost anyway.

Now he was clear again, and only his heels brushed the rock face as he crawled higher. And now he could hear a new sound, the restless brushing of the waves against the cliffs. He was all but there. And now, too, the passage suddenly lost its upward slope, and became almost easy to crawl along. Yet it was narrowing again, and he was forced to remain on his belly and worm himself forward, on and on, until without warning he saw a lighter patch in front of him, and a moment later his head pushed through an opening and he gazed at the night.

He was about seventy feet up, he figured, on the most vertical part of the cliff, looking down at the white foam from each of the gentle waves which hit the base, and still opposite the big yacht. She remained at anchor, and there were lights burning on deck and in the downstairs saloon. The searchlight also burned, playing on the entrance to the cave, some distance to his right, and also occasionally sweeping over the rock face to either side. *Esmeralda* was moored beside the accommodation ladder.

The light was not a problem at this moment; this hole was no more than a dark pin point in the cliff. But the sea was. He could not stand up for a proper dive, carrying himself away from the rock wall. He would have to drop like a stone, which involved the risk of being caught by a wave and thrown against the jagged teeth before he could regain control of himself. Nor could he tell from up here if there were any rocks close enough beneath the surface to break his legs as he came down.

He sighed, twisted on to his back, and cautiously pushed his shoulders out of the hole to look up. But there was no joy there. The wall was as sheer as ever, and stretched another hundred feet and more above him. He'd need proper climbing equipment and a support team to get up there.

So it was just a matter of evaluating the odds. If he worked his way back down into the cavern, supposing he could do that, he might find another way out. He *might*. But he could not get back down before daylight, which would make leaving impossible for another twelve hours. And that would be too long for the Prince. If he jumped from up here, he might well kill himself right off. But they had noticed no underwater heads as they had swum towards the cliff the previous night; he was a long way from the spit. Nor was the sea particularly large at this moment; it was indeed a very gentle swell. Therefore the risk was acceptable, in cold terms.

Therefore once again he had to subdue the fear which was eating at his belly, sapping his resolution. This could only be done here by a touch of the finalities. So, he must believe either that he would be killed outright in the fall, or that he would survive it unharmed. As simple as that. One or the other. One which meant the end of everything, and thus of all problems. And the other which meant that Wilde would go on, and on, and on.

Suddenly it occurred to him that he did not much care either way which result it was. It was some time since he had felt that way. But in the old days, it had been that carelessness of life or death which had made him so deadly.

Wilde put his hands on the lip of the hole, thrust his strength down, and hurled his body away from the cliff.

CHAPTER 9

By arching his body as soon as he was clear, Wilde managed to turn a complete somersault and get his feet down. Then there was just time to fill his lungs and clamp the forefinger and thumb of his right hand on to his nose before he broke the water. Now he thrust his feet out as soon as they were beneath the surface, to bring his body round in another arc, and yet he struck something—probably the sand at the bottom, he thought—a paralysing blow with his hip and felt as if the entire top had been lifted off his head as he gained the surface again.

For all the noise inside his brain, he had no idea how much of a splash he had created. Something, certainly; the spotlight left the cliff face and drifted across the sea, pin-pointing the spreading ripples where he had entered. But by now he was already much farther out, treading water, only his eyes showing. There was some shouting on the deck of the ship, but it did not last very long, and within a few minutes the spotlight returned to its watch on the rock face. They had decided that it must have been a jumping fish.

He approached the huge hull, using a breast stroke. The motor cruiser continued to nod at the foot of the accommodation ladder, but there was no prospect of getting on board her; someone sat in the gangway of *Female Spirit,* with a rifle across his or her knees.

Presumably there would be others awake; he had no idea how many people were now on board. His only hope was to cause so much distraction that he would become just another nuisance.

Cautiously he raised his head, checked the breeze. It was off the land, and gentle. But sufficient to move a fibre-glass motor boat; for the moment the mist had cleared, but no doubt it would return with the dawn.

He dived, went deep into the darkness of the bay, swam forward, and came up under the stern of *Female Spirit.* Here he could see the warp securing the stern of *Esmeralda*. It was drooping as it descended from the deck of the larger ship, and was only a couple of feet above his head where it dipped on to the aft cleat of the motor boat. He eased himself forward, grasped the side of the smaller boat, and cautiously worked the clove hitch free.

Now *Esmeralda* was held only by her bow, but that was where the breeze was coming from. The stern would begin to drift out soon enough, but sufficiently slowly, he trusted, not to alarm a sleepy guard whose attention was in any event focussed on the distant cliff face.

Wilde dived again, found his way along *Esmeralda*'s hull, came up at the bow. This was not going to be so easy; the warp had already hardened, and was five feet clear of the water. It would be too risky to try to draw himself up; he could only hope that the stern would stay put for another five minutes.

He swam forward to reach the bow of *Female Spirit*. A moment later he was gratefully resting, he legs wrapped round the steel links of the anchor chain. His last moment of safety, because the moment he swung himself up he would be a sitting target. But it was already past four, and dawn was only a couple of hours off. He'd be even more exposed then.

Besides, he had to get on deck before the guard noticed that the stern of the motor boat was free.

He reached up, locked his fingers on the links, and pulled himself from the water. No point in thinking now. He had to go steadily upwards, hand over hand over hand, and ignore the pain biting into his fingers, the weary agony at his shoulders, the emptiness of his belly, the helplessness of his legs waving to and fro. And what a goddamned long chain this was.

His swinging feet brushed the bow of the yacht, and he paused to control his breathing before putting his right hand up to grasp the rail. A moment later he crouched in the darkness of the fore deck, watching the lights of the saloons and the wheelhouse. Nothing moved.

Cautiously he crawled aft along the port scupper, reached the cleat to which *Esmeralda*'s bow warp was fastened. It took him only a moment to release the various reverse turns, and he left the rope loose around the cleat, then stretched the remainder across the deck.

He had about ten seconds, he calculated; the rope was already slipping with every gentle bob of the motor boat.

He slithered away from the rail, arrived next to the wheelhouse door, tried to make himself a part of the shadow drifting away from the flying bridge, and waited.

The splash of the rope entering the water sounded like a gunshot in the stillness of the night.

"Steve?" A voice from immediately above him, as he had feared. A man's voice, vaguely familiar.

"I heard it," Steve called.

"Steve?"

Wilde had a feeling that he had poked a stick into an ants' nest. This was Madeleine, emerging from the saloon aft. He could see her clearly, silhouetted against the light; she carried a rifle. And Steve certainly carried a rifle. And no doubt the man above him as well. And they were all very much awake.

"What was it, Steve?" Madeleine said over the side.

"Can't see anything," Steve said. "Maybe another of those fish jumping. I mean, what else could it be?"

Movement from above; the man was leaning on the rail of the bridge, looking down; Wilde could only pray that he remained no more than a shadow within a shadow.

"If you're so sure they're in there for good, Madeleine, why don't we just push off? Staying here is too damned hard on the nerves."

"Then pull yourself together," Madeleine said. "What is there to be nervous about? We're holidaying, aren't we? We'll leave when Clem says so. And he wants to have a look at that cliff in daylight, just to make sure there aren't any possible escape holes. So stop worrying."

"But keep awake," the man grumbled. "Yeah, yeah, yeah."

He moved from the rail, and Madeleine went back inside. Wilde could allow himself to breathe again. But his problems seemed to be multiplying. Three here, and then the mysterious Clem, and Carmel Wane, no doubt nursing her wounded shoulder, and Jonquil Malone . . . and how many others? And what had happened to Bruno della Guardia? Or was he also one of them?

But at least it seemed to be established that Clem was in command.

The night was again quiet. Correction, the morning. It would be light in little over an hour. The last hour of his life? How goddamned stupid could one get. He was risking his neck for a man he did not like, for a regime he actively disliked, for a cause in which he had no great interest.

Risking his neck? He was giving it away.

"Hey," Steve yelled. *"Esmeralda*'s loose."

"What?" The man above him was back at the rail, and then running aft for the ladder.

Another shout came from aft; Madeleine. Wilde reached up for the wheelhouse door, depressed the catch, and slid the door back along its track, waiting for the squeal. But *Female Spirit* was a new ship and in good condition; the track was greased, and the door made no sound. Wilde wormed inside and very gently pulled it shut behind him. Aft was a confused mass of shouting people. But he had not yet even begun distracting them; he had no chance of calling Ajaccio and not being discovered—he had to foresee what might happen afterwards as well. Carefully he flicked the cut-out switch on the alarm system.

The door into the lobby was open, as was the door into the bar. On the settee in the swimming saloon beyond someone was still asleep, but Wilde could not identify it beneath the blanket. Maybe it was Jonquil. He was tempted to step in there and deal with her right away; she remained at the top of his list.

But the chance was already gone. Before he could move Madeleine ran in from aft, still carrying her rifle.

"Clem," she shouted. "Clem, wake up. *Esmeralda*'s worked herself loose and drifted away, and carried the tender with her."

Wilde slid out of the door and on to the spiral staircase; his bare feet made no sound on the steel steps. Below decks the ship was still, except for the hum of the generator. He reached the engine-room level, listened at the door leading forward. This was closed and bolted. He was tempted to unlock it now; there *would* be a useful diversion. But one which could backfire; he did not know how many of the crew were capable of movement, or if any of them were in the plot against their prince.

On the other hand, supposing they were loyal, he was gambling with their lives as well as his own. Life was like that.

He opened the door to the engine room, closed it behind him, was surrounded by the hum. He switched on the lights; the brilliance dazzled him for several seconds. Then he went aft to the tool room, found himself a large screwdriver, returned to the engine room, and lay on the cat walk between the two huge General Motors diesels. Beneath each engine was the sea-cock which allowed the salt water to enter and circulate in its jacket round the outside of the engine itself, exchanging its heat for that of the sealed fresh water system which cooled the block, before being expelled over the side from the wet exhaust. The cocks were controlled by two small wheels, and these Wilde turned off before getting to work with his screwdriver to disconnect the thick rubber linking hose. It took him several minutes to free the starboard pipe, and another ten to free the port. Already water was seeping past the valve and dripping into the bilges.

He turned to the pumps. It was again a simple matter to disconnect the hoses with his screwdriver. Now any water sucked out of the bilges would merely be deposited back again. Once he turned on the cocks, *Female Spirit* would slowly fill. Unless something was done about it.

Wilde turned the first wheel, watched the water start to flow, turned the other wheel, and made a hasty calculation. At the rate the sea was coming in he figured that in about an hour the ship would have started to settle.

His last task was to use the screwdriver to pierce and rip the two lengths of intake hose he had removed. Even if he was immediately overpowered, and the crew discovered what was wrong and closed the cocks, they would not be able to run the engines for more than a few minutes before they would overheat. He switched off the lights, went to the door, and listened. The swish of the water pouring into the hull seemed unnaturally loud. He stepped through, closed the door behind him. The sound of the water dwindled beneath the hum of the generator; that would go in about half an hour, he reckoned, as the sea reached the batteries. Time enough.

He crouched in the lobby, once again listening. There was noise on deck, but down here the ship was as still as before, a huge floating palace of steel and mahogany and teak. Now with a mortal wound in its belly.

He climbed the spiral staircase, quickly and silently, reached the upper deck. The saloons were empty. Most of the voices seemed to be trying to persuade each other to swim after *Esmeralda*.

Wilde went into the wheelhouse, closed and locked the door. He switched on the transmitter, waited for it to warm up, and turned the crystal turner to two one eight two kilocycles, the distress frequency. He picked up the microphone, and pressed the button.

"Mayday, mayday, mayday," he said. "Mayday, mayday, mayday. *Female Spirit, Female Spirit, Female Spirit* calling all stations. I am sinking, at anchor in the north end of the Gulf of Porto. I say again, I am sinking at anchor, in the north end of the Gulf of Porto. In addition, two members of my crew have got lost on a pot-holing expedition ashore. The mouth of a cave has fallen in and trapped them. I need help urgently. Mayday, mayday, mayday. *Female Spirit, Female Spirit, Female Spirit* calling all stations."

He flicked the button.

"*Female Spirit, Female Spirit, Female Spirit,*" said a tired voice. "I do not understand your message, *Female Spirit*. Ajaccio Radio, Ajaccio Radio, Ajaccio Radio, calling *Female Spirit*. I do not understand your message. Will you say again please, and restate your position. Over."

"The north end of the Gulf of Porto," Wilde said. "I cannot be more accurate than that. But it is urgent that help comes at once. My pumps are out of action and my engine room is filling. Do you read me, Ajaccio Radio? Over."

There was an explosion behind him. He turned, watched the glass panel in the door shattering. He figured he had only a few seconds to live, and dropped to his knees to present less of a target.

"*Female Spirit, Female Spirit, Female Spirit,*" said the tired voice. "We will send a lifeboat to the Gulf of Porto. But I do not understand the message about people being trapped on shore. Would you say again, please?"

Another explosion. They had stopped shooting, and were swinging their rifle butts to break the lock.

"Ajaccio Radio," Wilde said. "Two people are trapped behind a rock-fall in a cave on shore, just a hundred feet north of my position. One of them is badly hurt. And I am being shot at. I need help desperately. I do not think the lifeboat alone will do. Send a gunboat as well, if you have one. Over."

Crash, bang, thump went the door behind him.

"I hope this is not a hoax, *Female Spirit*," Ajaccio Radio remarked. "We are sending help as quickly as we can. Ajaccio Radio, over and out."

"Female Spirit, Female Spirit, Female Spirit," came another voice. *"Dingo* here. I say, is that you, Wilde?"

"My God," Wilde said. "Smith Horton?"

"Wilde?" Smith Horton asked again. "Do identify yourself, old man. It so happens that I think I can probably reach you as quickly as the lifeboat. Do confirm, old chap. Over."

Wilde thumbed the button. "In case of need," he said. "I always think of Smith Horton." He watched the door swinging inwards, the muzzle of a rifle swinging in his direction. "Make haste, old chum. Wilde over and out."

ii

Someone fired. The bullet smashed into the radio set with a crackling crunch which was followed by a cloud of smoke. Wilde, falling across the wheelhouse, did not suppose his respite would last for very long.

But Madeleine had recognised him. "Don't shoot," she told the men with her. "Wilde."

He sat up, and rubbed the back of his head where he had banged it. He gazed at Madeleine, carrying a rifle, and at Steve, carrying a rifle. And at Bunty, carrying a rifle.

"The gang's all here," he said. "I *thought* I recognised your voice."

"And I thought you would prove more trouble than we hoped," Bunty said.

"But how the hell did you get here?" Wilde asked.

Bunty merely grinned. "We'd be better off if he were dead, Madeleine," he suggested, his finger curling on the trigger.

Madeleine smiled. "Oh no. Not yet, Bunty. I have lots of things I want to do to him. Besides, he has so many things to tell us. What were you doing here, Jonas?"

"Calling Ajaccio," Wilde explained. "I thought we could do with some of the *gendarmerie*. They're on their way. I understand there are some of the Foreign Legion stationed in Corsica as well."

Madeleine's smile started to freeze. "And what about Prince Walid? And Halma?"

"They're still in the cave," Wilde said. "The old boy has a bullet in the leg, don't you know, and is in no proper condition for climbing up and down rocks. And Halma naturally volunteered to stay with him."

Madeleine frowned at him. "You expect us to believe that?"

"I never lie, sweetheart. It makes life so very complicated."

"We know the Prince was hurt," Bunty said.

Madeleine continued to frown. "And so they sent Wilde out to try to get help. And I suppose it was you cast off *Esmeralda?*"

"It seemed like a good idea, at the time . . ."

"But if help is coming . . ." Bunty said.

"They won't know where to look," Steve pointed out. "If they find an empty bay, they will think it was a hoax."

"So if we just up anchor and leave . . ." Madeleine said thoughtfully.

"We can be miles away at sea by the time any boat can get up here from Ajaccio," Bunty said. "All we have to do is pick up Clem. And the Prince will stay buried, with his little playmate. At least he should die happy."

Madeleine smiled. "And we will have Wilde. It should be an enjoyable cruise. But we must hurry. Bunty, get the engines started. Steve, call Clem back. No, I'll do it. You hold the gun on Wilde."

"Don't tell me your boss is swimming after *Esmeralda?*" Wilde asked. "What a gallant fellow."

But she had already left.

"Would you care to start crawling?" Steve asked. "Don't even dream of getting up, or I shall put a bullet where it will hurt most. And you won't even die very quickly."

Wilde didn't think the time was right for argument. He shifted on to his hands and knees, crawled for the door. Bunty was already fiddling with the controls. From aft he could hear Madeleine shouting at the man named Clem. The starboard engine roared into life.

"Keep going," Steve said from behind him. "Into the saloon. I know you can mix us all a cocktail. What is the matter, Bunty?"

"It does not sound right." A moment later the port engine also blared forth. "This one too."

"Stop there, Wilde," Steve said. "What do you mean, it does not sound right?"

"I do not know," Bunty grumbled. Wilde looked over his shoulder. Steve was distracted, but not that distracted. The rifle still pointed at the base of his spine.

Bunty shrugged. "But they are going. Once we are out at sea I can stop them and have a look. Now, let me see, the fans." He pulled a switch. "And the alarm system has been turned off. These Xandans are a careless bunch." He flicked another switch, and the alarm blared as the red light glowed.

"What in the name of God is that?" Steve demanded.

Bunty stooped to peer at the dial. "Bilge," he announced. "There is too much water in the bilge. That would account . . ." He snapped the switch on the electric bilge pumps. "She must have a leak."

"A leak?" Steve demanded, his voice suddenly high.

"It can only be a slight leak," Bunty said reassuringly. "After all, we have been in command of the ship for ten hours, and we have noticed nothing. The water can only just have reached danger level. It should take only a few minutes to pump her dry."

"Then why is the light still glowing?" Steve wanted to know. "You had better get down there now."

"Maybe." Bunty turned back from the console, and Wilde rolled over and kicked. His toes caught Steve behind the knee, and he fell with an exclamation of alarm. The rifle exploded and shattered the radar display unit. Bunty had also fallen, and Wilde hit him with a short arm jab. Then he reached for Steve before he could get the rifle up again, but Bunty had recovered and seized him by the arm, while Steve now kicked in turn. His toes caught Wilde on the chest, and he fell backwards out of the wheelhouse, taking Bunty with him. For a moment they teetered at the top of the spiral staircase, then he lost his balance completely. Bunty gave a shout, and a moment later they were tumbling down the stairs, rolling and bumping. The rifle plummeted to the deck below.

Wilde found himself on the dining level, looking up at Steve, who was coming down. But Bunty was already opening the engine-room door. Wilde grasped the banisters and hurled himself downwards, reached the lowest level, found himself in a couple of inches of water, slowly seeping over the engine-room sill.

Bunty had switched on the light, was staring in horror at the flooding engines when he heard the splash of Wilde's arrival. He turned and came back, throwing punches from every direction. "Come on, Steve," he bellowed.

Wilde grappled for him, got him round the neck, and was hit a paralysing blow in the belly, which brought his stomach up to his mouth and had him back on his knees. Steve came clattering down the steps, and Wilde realised that between them they might just prove too much for him, in this confined space and in his state of near exhaustion. Desperately he pulled away from Bunty and fell through the engine-room door; the generator still hummed reassuringly, but there was water everywhere. Bunty seemed to be sitting astride his legs, swinging his clenched fists.

Wilde rolled, and Bunty fell over. Wilde scrabbled at the bolt to the engine-room door, and gazed at Steve. He had picked up the rifle and now thrust it forward. Wilde slammed the door on the muzzle and pushed the bolt home, then sank to his knees against it, to pant, and feel water splashing at his thighs, and attempt to think, in the roar of the engines to either side.

The hands were back, clawing at his waist. Wilde turned, and brought his own arms round in a gigantic bear hug, sweeping Bunty's hands into his sides and bringing him close. Then he left one hand to do the pinioning, and with the other searched for his throat. His fingers closed on Bunty's windpipe, and he gagged.

"Listen," Wilde shouted. "If you don't stop behaving like a lunatic, I'll feed you into the engines."

Bunty subsided. The wheels of the alternators were only inches away from them, and even idling the engines were making some five hundred revolutions a minute; without the cooling water being able to circulate they were already starting to smell hot, and above even that there came the tang of steam where the water was beginning to lap at the overheated blocks.

The sea was up to their waists. Wilde wondered how high the battery boxes were situated.

The gun butt smashed against the door outside, but the door was made of steel.

"She's sinking," Bunty said, as if he had just realised it.

"Could happen," Wilde agreed.

"But how . . . you?"

"I figured I'd need some help."

"To drown?"

"Nobody will drown," Wilde told him. "If everybody is prepared to be sensible. Care to chat?"

Bunty glared at him, while Steve went bang, bang, bang on the door. But suddenly the noise stopped. A moment or two later the engines stopped as well. The silence was positively deafening, because the generator had also stopped; the only sound was the steady gurgle of water entering the hull. And then the light went off.

iii

"Oh, Christ," Bunty grumbled. "They've cut out."

"No, they haven't," Wilde said. "Diesel engines will run as long as the air intake is above water, and these are a long way from being covered. Someone's pulled the stop buttons. I figure they want to negotiate."

"What's there to negotiate?" Bunty asked.

"Our lives. Which are now in some danger. I tell you what. If you don't want to drown, really, just take a deep breath and go down and turn those sea-cocks shut."

"My God," Bunty said. "You mean . . . ?"

"Simple as that."

Bunty inhaled, held his breath, and ducked under the starboard engine. Wilde listened to him scrabbling about in the bilge, then he re-emerged and gasped for breath. "You must be stark, raving mad."

"There's another one," Wilde reminded him.

"Wilde," Steve called from beyond the door. "Are you still there, Wilde?"

"Of course he's still here," Bunty shouted.

"Are you all right?" Steve asked.

"Yes, I'm all right," Bunty snapped. "What about the others?"

"They're back on board," Steve said. "But Clem didn't get *Esmeralda*. She's still drifting out to sea."

"Don't bother about her now," Bunty said. "Wilde wants to do a deal."

"I hate to interrupt," Wilde said. "But if you don't turn off that other cock, there isn't going to be anything to bargain about."

"Bloody hell," Bunty grumbled, but he went under.

"You still there?" Steve called. "What about your terms."

"My terms?" Wilde asked. "I want your surrender."

"You have got to be joking. We can just sail this boat away from here."

"Not while she's sinking you can't. If I turn these cocks back on she'll go down in half an hour."

"If you sink her down there, you will also die," Steve pointed out.

"That goes with the job. I'll have a lot of fun company."

There was an explosion from the darkness beside him as Bunty surfaced. But the water continued to gurgle.

"God," he gasped.

"You'll have to try again," Wilde said. "And I wouldn't leave it too long."

"I can't," Bunty shouted, his voice afraid. "Don't you understand? I can't."

"You can't turn that little wheel?"

"I can turn it," Bunty panted. "But then it sticks. It just stops, before shutting off the water."

"Oh, damn and blast," Wilde said. He ducked his head and went down. His hands scrabbled over the various pipes leading away from the wheel and then found the wheel itself. He twisted it round, but it would not turn. The wrong way, surely. He tried the other way, and it moved freely enough. But the flow of water increased. Desperately he thrust both hands down, found the filter which filled the centre of the piping, pulled on it. It would not come away. He got two fingers inside, found the end of a branch. Of all the really foul luck, that he would have opened the intake as a piece of tree was floating by.

He got his head above the surface.

"Got you," Steve said, reaching for his neck, while Bunty tried to hold his arms; he had opened the door to let his friend in.

"Don't be childish," Wilde snapped. "There's a branch jammed in the filter."

Bunty released him. "Christ Almighty," he said. "Can't you free it?"

"Given time. It would be simpler to reconnect the hoses. I destroyed the originals, but there must be spares, somewhere. So switch the lights back on."

"The batteries are dead," Steve said. "That's why I came back down."

"Oh, Christ," Bunty said. "The hand pump won't stop this flow now."

"So get the engines started," Steve said. "Drive us round the headland and on to the beach."

Bunty sighed. "I need electricity, to start this lot up again."

"For God's sake," Steve shouted, also beginning to sound afraid. "Does the whole bloody world need electricity?"

"That is what this mix-up is all about," Wilde reminded him. "There's a life raft."

"And where does that leave us when the coast guard arrive?"

"One really has to think of all these aspects of a situation, before embarking on an adventure like this," Wilde said. "I think you should at least start work with the hand pump. I'll come back for you."

By now he had made sure where they both were.

"Stop him," Bunty shouted.

But Wilde was already banging their heads together, and they went into the water in a splutter and a wail. He waded past them, closed the door, and slipped the outside bolt. They wouldn't drown for the next ten minutes, he figured, but the water was already knee deep in the lobby, and acidic smells were coming from the deep freeze, while the darkness was utter.

And now there were shouts of alarm from the crew's quarters. Wilde pulled the bolt on the door, bumped into someone who immediately threw both arms around his chest.

"For God's sake," Wilde shouted. "You must be Zahir."

The man pushed him against the bulkhead and tried to get his fingers round his throat.

"Don't you understand English?" Wilde begged, and hit him in the belly.

Zahir gave a groan and sank to his knees with a splash.

"Mr. Wilde? Is that you?" Captain Albarana, his voice muffled through the bandage swathing his head.

"Where are you?"

"In my cabin, Mr. Wilde."

Wilde staggered forward, wrenched open the door. Behind him he heard Zahir splashing to his feet.

"Call off the dog, will you?" he said. "I've come to help."

Albarana said something in Arabic. But Wilde could still hear the sailor breathing, just behind him.

"Where is the Prince?" Albarana demanded.

"Safe for the time being," Wilde said. "But this ship is sinking."

"Sinking?" Albarana cried. "But how?"

"I opened the sea-cocks," Wilde explained. "It's a long story. How many are you?"

"There are seven of us down here, Mr. Wilde."

There was no time for mathematics; the number seemed about right. "Do you think you can get your men on deck? You can use one of the life rafts."

"I can try, Mr. Wilde. But I do not understand . . ."

"Don't try. But take it easy coming up until you are sure the coast is clear. Or you may get your head shot off. Give me five minutes."

He figured it would take that long for them to get organised. He splashed back into the lobby, dropped to his hands and knees, and felt in the water. There was no sound from behind the engine-room door; it had occurred to them to look for the emergency way out.

His fingers touched the rifle. He picked it up and started up the spiral staircase. Now he had the best odds since this mess began. But it was surprising that neither Madeleine nor the man they called Clem had come down to see what was happening. And he still did not know what had happened to Jonquil.

There was something else troubling him as well, but for the moment he couldn't decide what it was.

But a moment later he got the answer to one of his questions. As he reached the dining level, he heard a recognisable high-pitched screaming from the cabins aft. He found his way through the saloon, now starting to assume an ominous list, and into the stateroom lobby. Most of the doors opened to his touch, but the last was locked, and it was from in here that the noise was coming.

"Stand clear," he bawled.

"Jonas," Jonquil shrieked. "Is that you, Jonas? Oh, thank God for that."

"Stay back," Wilde said, pointed the rifle muzzle at the lock, and squeezed the trigger. When he kicked the door a moment later it swung inwards.

Here the darkness was more intense than ever. He fumbled towards the bunks, found her, still wearing her bikini, tied hand and foot.

"Jonas Wilde." Her voice sounded distinctly discontented with life. "Where have you *been?*"

He fumbled at her wrists. "Busy."

"Ugh. You're all wet."

Her feet were also free. "That is because this ship is sinking."

"Sinking?" Her voice rose again, and both her arms went round his neck.

"Yes," Wilde said. "You and I have a good deal of talking to do, but right now there isn't time. Are you hurt in any way?"

"I've a bump on the head."

"You have always had a bump on the head," he pointed out. "It happened when you fell out of your pram, remember? If it wasn't that it would be an awful waste of time to drown someone I intend to murder myself, slowly, I'd leave you here. Now get down forward and help Captain Albarana evacuate his crew. Most of them aren't feeling very well."

"But I can't see."

"Then fumble a bit."

"But . . . what about . . . ?"

"I wish I knew."

"Jonas." She held his arm still. "They were down here just now. They came to get Carmel. She isn't very well."

"That figures." As he had suspected, they had deserted the rank and file.

"Jonas. I didn't let you down. Honest. It all happened so quickly."

"All right, sweetheart. All right." Gently he disengaged himself from her fingers. "The captain needs help." He went to the door.

"But the Prince, Jonas," she wailed. "What happened to the Prince?"

"He'll be around." Wilde ran outside, back through the dining room, heard the grunts and pants of the crew feeling their way up the stairs.

"Stay with it," he said, reached the upper level, suddenly almost light after the utter darkness below decks, and was sent tumbling back down by a bullet which screamed through the saloon to shatter the wheelhouse windows. But this time he did not let go of the rifle. "Take cover," he snapped down the steps, and wormed his way back up the stairs.

He poked his head into the lobby. Now there was a definite list, and above the sounds of the men on the stairs, to which had been added Jonquil's voice, there were bumps and crashes and splintering noises as various objects became dislodged by the cant. There was a real likelihood that the vessel would turn on her side as she went down, because only one of the sea-cocks was open and the main rush of water was settling in the port compartments.

He rose to his knees, and once again an explosion seared the grey light of the approaching dawn, sent him flat to the floor again. But now he had ascertained that the gunman was in the doorway to the swimming saloon. He turned his own weapon in that direction, waited for a movement, and fired three times. There was a scream and a crash as the shots echoed around the ship. Wilde leapt to his feet and ran, throwing himself to the floor in the doorway, next to the dead body of Steve. But the rifle had been removed, and he could see Bunty in the deck doorway. He immediately squeezed the trigger again, to be greeted by a most unpleasant click.

"Well, Mr. Wilde," Bunty said. "The end of the affair, eh?"

"I'd still like to know how you got here," Wilde said, keeping low.

"I flew. I left the moment you had picked up your suitcases."

And landed at either Bastia or Ajaccio, presumably. But how had he got *here?* It occurred to Wilde that there were just too many damned imponderables in this situation. But time to think was the one thing he did not possess. Already he was rolling again, over and over to the side of the saloon, as Bunty's rifle was exploding again. He heard the crump of the bullet smashing into the floor where he had just been lying.

Then he was on his knees, and his feet, and hurling his own empty weapon at the doorway. Bunty fired again, at the dark object he saw sailing through the air. His rifle was still pointing upwards as Wilde connected with his waist. They fell together, Bunty tumbling over backwards. He pulled the trigger again, but this time it was his turn to hear the click of an empty magazine.

Wilde rose to his knees above the fallen man, and swung the back of his hand. Bunty moaned, but he was far from out. His arms came forward to encircle Wilde's body, and a tremendous amount of strength was being generated into his arms and shoulders as he squeezed. For a moment the morning turned into a kaleidoscope of brilliantly flashing lights before Wilde's eyes, then he got himself back under control, locked his hands together, and brought them down with all his strength on the back of Bunty's neck.

Bunty grunted, but his arms did not relax. Wilde had to hit him twice more before the weight suddenly slid away from his body and hit the deck.

"Jonas?" Jonquil called from behind him. "Are you there, Jonas?"
"I'm here," Wilde said. "Up you come."

He forced himself to his feet, staggered on deck. Already the dawn mist was gathering over the hills around him, shrouding everything in a clammy white, bringing visibility down to a few yards. He could not even see the cliffs, now. But he could hear a reassuring chatter, from astern of him, followed by the "blaaagh" of a fog-horn.

He ran back into the steadily lightening saloon, pushed his way past stumbling sailors in bandages and splints, crashed into the wheel-house, tore open the lockers to find a Very pistol. He returned aft with a handful of cartridges, fired three flares into the mist.

"Ahoy," he shouted. "Ahoy there. What ship is that?"

"Ahoy," came the reply from very close. "My ship is the *Dingo*. We are looking for a ship called *Female Spirit,* reported to be in distress in this area."

"Smith Horton, you splendid fellow," Wilde shouted. "We are in fact about to sink. Stand by to pick up survivors."

CHAPTER 10

The trawler nosed close alongside, away from the list, which was becoming more and more pronounced. The clinometer in the wheelhouse was showing twenty-five degrees and edging over all the time; it was even difficult to stand.

"No warps," Smith Horton shouted. "I don't want to be dragged under. How on earth did you let her go so far, Wilde?"

"It has always been my ambition to scuttle a quarter-of-a-million-pound job," Wilde said. "They say everything comes to him who waits. Now come along chaps, hurry it up. Give them a hand, Jonquil."

"I wish I knew what's happening," she grumbled, and peered through the mist at Smith Horton. "You could have come sooner. Good morning, Martha."

They sounded like old friends. It occurred to Wilde that perhaps they *were* old friends.

"Let's get those men on board," Martha Smith Horton said. "My God, but what happened to them?"

Jonquil assisted Splendide over the rail. "People always look like this after knowing Wilde for an hour or two. You just don't know how lucky you've been."

Wilde left them to it, crouched beside Bunty, shook him back into wakefulness.

"Listen to me," he said. "You have only minutes to live, unless you co-operate. Where would Madeleine and this fellow Clem have gone?"

"Ashore," Bunty muttered. "They swam, with Carmel."

"You mean they deserted you?"

"It is their business to preserve the group," Bunty said. "The group comes first, the individuals come second. A life is of no concern, providing the group is eternal. For what . . ."

"Okay, okay, okay," Wilde said. "We put out a propaganda of our own, and it is equally boring." The mist would clear, when the sun got at it. One hour, two? Yet they would have had a long swim to the beach. They would hardly have got there yet, hampered by Carmel. "Did they have weapons?" He gave Bunty a shake.

"They took two of the rifles," Bunty said. "They tied them to a life-belt."

Wilde glanced along the deck. Three of the life-belts were missing from their brackets. But Carmel would have needed one.

"One more question, Bunty. Where would they be going? I mean, would they have a destination in mind?"

Bunty stared at him.

"Now don't let's get all nasty and unco-operative," Wilde said. "We are going to get them no matter where they go. You can save us some time and trouble, that's all."

"They have gone ashore," Bunty said. "That is all I know."

"Jonas," Jonquil said at his elbow. "Smith Horton says he can't wait any longer."

"Then give a hand with the boy." Between them they humped Bunty to his feet, dragged him to the rail. Now there was a distinct area of topside to be crossed before the trawler could be reached, and Smith Horton was looking anxious.

"Throw us some lines," Wilde shouted.

Martha obliged, and he hastily tied bowlines around each of their waists. "Slide," he commanded.

They climbed over the rail, and slipped down the smooth paint towards the keel, which was already starting to show. Smith Horton gave a touch on his port engine, and the trawler moved away to safety. Wilde re-entered the water, and heard a gasp from Jonquil as she fell beside him. But almost immediately they were dragged clear by Zahir and Captain Albarana.

Wilde sat on the deck and panted, and gazed at *Female Spirit*. Now he could see the great bronze propellers, and acres of anti-fouling on her hull, and now too, ironically, the exits for the various sea-cocks, including the starboard entry into the engine room.

"Do you know," Smith Horton remarked beside him. "I have never seen a ship sink before."

"I have," Wilde said. "Too damned many." Someone pressed a towel into his hand, and he dried himself, all the while gazing at *Fe-*

male Spirit. Now she went with a rush. Someone must have left a porthole open well down in the hull, and water was pouring into the ship from several directions. Now too they could hear the crashings and bangings from within the ship as everything cut loose. Wilde glanced at Captain Albarana. The captain came to attention, hands at his side, and then saluted as ever more of his ship's hull showed.

Then she went, in a cloud of spray and steam, seeming to turn almost right over and then stopping suddenly, while the morning filled with the grind of steel and timbers.

"The bridge has hit bottom," Albarana muttered.

But the hull was settling too. The spray bubbled, and sent breakers pounding against the cliff face. Just for a moment. Then there was a sudden immense silence, with only ripples disturbing the surface of the bay, while the mist gathered ever more thickly about them.

ii

"Makes you want to weep," Jonquil said.

"Yes," Wilde agreed. "I wonder if you could take us a little closer in, Smith Horton, old boy?"

"Well, I don't know about that," Smith Horton said, peering into the mist. "I think the best thing I can do is anchor and wait for this to clear. It never hangs about more than a couple of hours. By that time, too, the coast guard may have turned up."

"And by that time the bosses of this outfit could be a hell of a long way away," Wilde said.

"You mean there are more?"

"You haven't even started yet," Wilde said. "Now look, ease slowly forward, steering about due east. There's a spit sticking out about two hundred yards in front of you, but that course should clear it. Once beyond you're in a wide, shallow bay. You can anchor there."

Smith Horton sighed. "Why sink one boat a day, when you can sink two? I must warn you that this is government property."

"So am I," Wilde reminded him. "Do you have any weapons on board this tub?"

Smith Horton eased the engine slow ahead, and the trawler slipped gently into the mist. "I have a pistol. But you're not going after those people alone? How many of them are there?"

"Two women and a man," Wilde said. "Not that I think sex comes into it very deeply."

"Armed?"

"With a couple of rifles, I understand. You want to alter course about two points to starboard."

Smith Horton jerked, stared at the rocks which had suddenly appeared on his port bow. "My God." He put the helm over. "I wish I knew exactly what was going on."

"So do I," Wilde said. He watched Jonquil coming out of the saloon aft. "Maybe this young lady can tell us. Everything under control?"

"If you can possibly call it that," she said. "Even Bunty is feeling a little depressed. Where are we going?"

"To pick up Clem and the girls."

"Ah," she said. "I like the sound of that. I'll help you."

"Oh no," Wilde said. "Oh no, no, no. I've had all of your help that I can possibly stand. I'm not even sure which side you were on."

"I was jumped," she said. "Believe me, it all happened so quickly I'm not sure myself. I was hit from behind. Feel here." She pressed his hand to her scalp. "That is a bump. And it hurts."

"Then you'd better go to bed."

Smith Horton was peering into his echo sounder. "I say, Wilde, old chap, I don't want to be a bore, but we have only eight feet." He put the engine into neutral.

Wilde looked aft. The rocks had disappeared. So had every evidence of land. But the beach had to be just over there. "So we'll anchor," he said, and went on deck.

"And then you're going ashore?" Smith Horton also came on deck.

"With your gun."

"And me, Jonas," Jonquil begged. "Listen. I'm in all kinds of trouble if this lot really have torn our system apart. My only hope is to bring them back."

"You make them sound like wild animals," Wilde said. "Listen, doll, this is not likely to be fun. In the first place, I don't have a clue where they have gone. In the second place, they will still outnumber us. In the third place, they have two rifles to our pistol. And in the fourth place, your business is to look after the Prince."

He released the brake on the winch, and the anchor plunged into the green water. The trawler obligingly came to a stop.

"My God," Smith Horton said. "The Prince. I'd forgotten about him."

"Happens all the time, to princes."

"But where is he? Don't tell me he's dead."

"Only buried," Wilde said. "But I'll imagine he'll survive for another hour or two. Now listen very carefully, old chap. When the coast guard turn up, tell them that Walid is in the cave just opposite where *Female Spirit* went down."

"But there isn't a cave where *Female Spirit* went down," Jonquil objected.

"There is," Wilde said patiently. "Madeleine blew in the entrance with dynamite. But it's there. And you can't help but see the fresh rock-fall if you look. Be a good chap and have something done about that, Smith Horton."

"Leave it to me," Smith Horton said. "I'll go and find that pistol, shall I?"

He hurried back into the wheelhouse, and Wilde pulled his ear. "He really is a most efficient fellow, you know."

"Oh, I do know," she said. "I mean, fancy *being* here, just when he was wanted." She gazed into the mist. "I don't see what we're supposed to accomplish. We don't even know where the beach is."

"Just so long as we know it's there." He went aft, untied the dinghy from its berth on the coach roof, and Jonquil helped him launch it. "Leave the outboard," he said. "The noise of that thing will travel for miles, and we don't really want them to know we're coming ashore."

Smith Horton reappeared on deck with a nine-millimetre Browning automatic pistol. "And here is your spare clip," he said. "Just in case you need it."

"You are an absolute treasure," Wilde agreed, and tucked the magazine into the waist-band of his trunks. "Let's go. That way."

There was a faint breeze, blowing the mist along, and more mist behind, unfortunately, but it would be coming down the pass between the hills, Wilde figured, which was the direction of the beach. He sat in the stern, and made sure the pistol was in working order, while Smith Horton rowed and Jonquil waited in the bows.

"Land ahead," she said, as if they had just crossed the Atlantic. Smith Horton backed his oars.

"Over you go," Wilde said. "It won't be as cold as it looks."

She sighed and daintily thrust one long leg into the water. Then her face relaxed. "It's quite warm, really. Come along, Jonas."

"I am with you." He also dropped into the waist-deep water. "Don't forget everything you have to do, old man," he told Smith Horton, and waded ashore to join Jonquil on the beach.

She was gazing at a discarded life-belt. "Well, what do you know," she said. "They did come this way, after all."

Wilde went to the tent. It remained exactly as they had left it the previous night. He stepped inside, looked around, rested his hand on the transmitter. It was not as cold as it should have been.

"Is this where they were hatched out?" Jonquil asked.

"Originally. Now they're on their way to a rendezvous with some-one or something."

"In that?" She watched the mist clouds come rolling down the hill to fill the valley and the bay; already Smith Horton had disappeared behind them, and there was no evidence that the trawler was there at all.

"They'll have followed the path," Wilde said. He could see the be-ginning of the beaten earth track, leading upwards. But Jonquil had taken only two steps when she stopped with a grunt.

"There are stones," she complained, standing on one leg and arch-ing her body this way and that to examine the other shapely instep.

"Paths often do," Wilde said. "I told you not to come."

He led her upwards, and the path grew steeper. They had to pick their way now between large and extremely unpleasant-looking peb-bles with jagged edges; even his feet were feeling the strain. And still the mist shrouded them, bathed them in clammy moisture, although now it was tinged with yellow to suggest that there was a sun, some-where, trying to get through.

But there was no evidence that anyone had walked this path be-fore them. Wilde was just beginning to wonder if they were on the right track, after all, when he saw a spot of dull brown coagulated dust in front of him.

"Carmel."

And a moment later they found her.

iii

Carmel Wane lay on her face on the stony earth; her fingers still bit into the ground, and blood was drifting away from the opened cut in her right shoulder—the bandage had come loose. She still wore a dressing gown, clinging damply to her body, wrapping itself round her legs. Her feet were bare, and also bleeding, and her hair wisped untidily.

"What a depressing sight," Jonquil said. "Is she dead?"

Wilde had already turned her over. "No. Just plumb wore out." He slapped her face, crisply, once and then twice.

Carmel's eyes flopped open. "Oh, God," she whispered.

"Isn't it strange," Jonquil remarked, "how people always say that when they see you?"

"Where are your friends?" Wilde asked.

"They wouldn't wait," Carmel muttered. "They wouldn't wait. Oh, God damn them. They wouldn't wait."

"How long ago?" Wilde asked.

She stared at him.

"You must make an effort, Carmel," Jonquil said.

Carmel's eyes moved from Wilde, and she seemed to notice Wilde for the first time. "I should have killed you, when I had the chance."

"I don't remember that you ever did. But the thought should serve to remind you that neither of us is particularly full of loving kindness towards you at this moment. If you don't tell me how long ago Clem and Madeleine left you, I might have to bang you about a little. And you look as if you have been sufficiently banged about for one day."

"Bastard." She searched her mouth and spat, but the spittle merely dribbled down her lip.

"If I let your head go," Wilde said. "It will fall on to a particularly nasty-looking stone. So, from a count of five: One, two, three . . ."

"I don't know," she said. "I fainted." But her left hand had twitched.

Wilde raised it, held the watch before her. "So when were they here?"

Her tongue circled her lips. "Five to seven."

The watch showed eleven minutes past. And the mist was clearing.

"Just what I wanted to hear. And what are they hoping to achieve, rushing about this particular part of Corsica?"

"I don't know."

"Oh, please, Carmel, be sensible. I know they used your radio."

"I don't know," she said. "They left me on the beach. Then they wanted me to walk up here."

Of course she was lying. But he really wasn't in the mood to rough her up. And he knew they could not be far in front of him. "Jonquil, this is going to lift in a couple of minutes. You help Carmel down to the beach, and give Smith Horton a shout."

"While you do what?"

"I think I should keep in touch with our friends, don't you?"

"*I* think you should come back with me, and wait for the gendarmerie."

"Which is likely to take a few hours yet, darling. And involve all sorts of other problems. Whereas my people can't be more than a mile away, at the moment. You just do as you are told, for once in your life."

Jonquil pouted. Carmel Wane groaned, and seemed about to faint.

"Have fun," Wilde said, and climbed the hill. He reached a crest as the sun came through the mist with a magical suddenness, whipping the white vapour to one side and leaving the red rock hills startlingly bare. In front of him the path dipped very gently into another valley, beyond which there was another range of hills. But those hills were at least half an hour away, and there was no one in the valley, unless they were lying down in the maqui scrub. Why should they do that?

To his left the ground also dipped, and then rose again, to the seaward cliffs. But these were almost bare, with no cover at all, except for a very old watch-tower, no doubt built by a Norman war-lord a few hundred years before, dominating the coast, able to withstand all but the most determined siege, and guarding the exit inland from the bay, to launch, if need be, a flank attack on any overconfident Saracen.

The only cover. Wilde did a hasty calculation. It was about half a mile away. Time enough for someone to reach it from here. And get his or her breathing back under control. And realise that this ridge was well within rifle range.

He looked back down the slope. The mist might have cleared from up here, but it was still obliterating the beach and the sea. The trawler was invisible, and Jonquil and Carmel Wane had disappeared on their journey back to the beach.

And he wore bathing trunks, with a pistol tucked into the waistband and a spare clip held in his left hand. He felt most remarkably naked.

There was nowhere else they could have gone. He began to trot towards the tower, shifting from foot to foot to present a constantly moving target, and keeping his gaze on the empty arrow slits, the gaping doorway. But the building remained silent in the growing light. Now his breathing came heavier, and for the first time he was really grateful for the week's training he had put in under Jonquil Malone and Bunty. Jonquil Malone. He still had not sorted that one out properly. And he had left Carmel Wane in her care, for the second time. But Carmel was unimportant when compared with the man called Clem.

And Madeleine. He had not forgotten Madeleine.

His muscles were also heavy, and his steps were laboured. He could not remember when last he had actually lain back and rested. For five minutes after Halma, for a couple of hours in the forepeak, was it only yesterday morning? But interspersed with those brief spells of exhausted inaction there had been utterly exhausting action, swimming, climbing, and physical encounter. He was feeling his age.

Behind him the sun cleared the mountains which form the backbone of Corsica, dispelling the last of the mist to make the morning suddenly hot, bringing the sweat tumbling from his face and shoulders, glinting from the upper window of the tower.

Glinting. Wilde half tripped and half fell as he left the path and threw himself to one side. Almost in the same instant he heard the crack of the rifle and watched the dust spurting. Clem had, after all, only been waiting for him to come close enough to be certain of killing him outright. And Clem had waited just a fraction of a second too long.

The rifle was exploding again and again and again, and dust was flying all around him. Wilde tried to glue himself into the earth, flattening every inch of his body, hoping he was as invisible as he felt. And counting. But Clem would have at least two shots left, he figured, even supposing he did not have a spare clip. And Madeleine had also taken a rifle, according to Bunty.

He moved his head, carefully, allowing his chin to rest on the ground while he peered through the bushes at the tower. It seemed to rise immediately in front of him, but he was at least fifty yards off. Say seven seconds to the doorway. Six seconds too long.

The sun played full on the weathered red stone. Carefully, inch by inch, Wilde brought up his right hand, holding the pistol. They could not stay there forever. They must know there was help on the way. They'd have to make sure he was dead, and then leave while they could. Time was on his side.

Except for the certainty that Clem was not a fool. Even if Wilde was dead, they were still faced with a walk of several hours to the nearest village. Several hours of walk over bleak headlands or empty hills, knowing that the police could move much faster than they.

That did not seem a very practicable proposition. After all, Clem had selected this bay himself as a rendezvous; this was the big one, when they were throwing everything they had got at the Prince. No matter how it turned out they would want to leave the set in a greater hurry than the speed afforded by *Esmeralda*. Because even *Esmeralda* could be chased and caught by a fast patrol vessel, or, more likely, by an aircraft.

Or even a helicopter. His head turned at the guttural whine, and he watched the small machine come sailing over the mountains behind him, searching for the flat earth immediately outside the castle.

Understanding crashed through his brain. Of how Bunty had managed to get from the airport to the ship, so quickly, and of why Clem and Madeleine had known they'd be able to beat the police to freedom. He swung the arm holding the pistol to his right, and squeezed the trigger as the helicopter touched the ground. He fired twice more, pumping bullets into the glass-walled cabin, unable to shatter the reinforced triplex but still sending streaks of cracking glass up and down the sides. The rotors, which had been slowly coming to rest, started to whirr again. Madeleine ran out of the doorway of the castle, shouting and waving. But the helicopter was already clear of the ground.

Wilde was on his feet and running, checking to fire twice more before he reached the dry moat which surrounded the tower and tumbled down its sides into the sludge at the bottom, rising to his knees and firing again, this time at Madeleine as she came to the edge of the parapet, her rifle thrust forward.

She disappeared, but he did not think she was hit. The helicopter was now some twenty feet above the ground, hovering, undecided whether it had fallen into a police trap or was indeed attacked by a single man.

Wilde leaned against the wall of the tower, which rose above him to a dizzy sixty feet, held his right wrist in his left hand, and took careful aim. He squeezed the trigger, once, twice, and the bullets screamed into the engine mounted aft as the aircraft slowly turned, and the pilot looked down. There was a flash of light. The noise of the explosion was lost in the crash as the aircraft struck the ground. The whoompff seemed to roar over his head, and even though he was protected by the sides of the moat the blast knocked him off balance.

He wondered what had happened to Madeleine, supposing she was still in the doorway. Desperately he released the empty clip, pulled it out of the butt of the pistol, slammed home the spare. He left the shelter of the wall, ran round the moat, and reached the banked earth before the doorway. Pistol thrust forward, he scrambled up, suddenly conscious of the immense heat rising from the burning helicopter only a few feet away; minor explosions continued to bang and snap and the whole machine gave off a loud crackling as it burned. The pilot was not to be seen; presumably he had died in the crash.

Wilde ran into the doorway, and checked. He had made no noise, with his bare feet, and against the background of sound. Madeleine lay on the earth floor, her rifle several feet away. Crouching beside her was Bruno della Guardia.

iv

"Why, Bruno," Wilde said. "What a pleasant surprise. I thought you were dead. Or something. Instead of which you've just changed names."

Leigh started to turn slowly.

"Keep it like that," Wilde requested. "How is Madeleine?"

"She is not dead," Leigh said, straightening, and gazing at the pistol.

"Can you carry her? I think it might be a good idea for us to return to the beach."

Leigh considered. "You are going to turn us over to the Prince?"

"I rather feel he deserves first crack, don't you?"

"If you don't mind," Leigh said, "I would prefer you to shoot me now. I think Madeleine would also prefer that."

"I agree it sounds unpleasant," Wilde said. "But I am assuming you took such a possibility into consideration before embarking on this little scheme. Would you like to lift the lady?"

Leigh hesitated, sighed, and shrugged. He turned, thrust one hand under Madeleine's knees and the other under her shoulders, straightened, turned, and threw her.

The oldest dodge in the world, and one at which Wilde himself was an expert. But there was a sting in the tail. Madeleine was not even unconscious. As Wilde side-stepped and moved backwards as well, her apparently flaccid body came to life. Her legs snaked for his neck, her hands went down to catch her fall, to take the weight of her body and throw it back in a vast hand-spring, which once again brought her legs booming at his face. Another hasty step backwards caught his heel in the rotting door, and he sat down heavily, Madeleine accumulating on his stomach.

Leigh was leaping for the rifle, and Wilde managed to send a shot in his general direction, but there was no prospect of aiming. And after that there was no prospect of doing anything more than wrestling with the snarling, spitting, scratching she-cat which had wrapped itself around him. Nails scraped down his face, knees bunched into his groin, elbows thudded into his chest, and snapping white teeth seemed designed for his eyes.

And for all the fury of her assault she knew exactly what she was doing. As his head jerked back to escape her nails her head swung round and her teeth dropped and sank into his right forearm. The pain was excruciating, and his muscles relaxed before he could summon any mental discipline, and his fingers opened. Madeleine's head came up, and her nails were back.

The pistol was gone. It was necessary to do something about the woman very quickly. Wilde brought his left hand into her back. He could not manage enough of a swing to hit her hard, so he closed his fingers on the flesh just above her buttocks, and squeezed and squeezed and squeezed. Madeleine was not the least fat; he was eating into flesh and muscle, with such a terrifying force that her head lolled and her mouth sagged, and her fingers lost their own power.

Wilde got the muscles of his right hand working again, and swung it sideways, cracking it into the base of her jaw, swinging her head over and driving the sense from her mind. She moaned, and flopped into semi-consciousness. Wilde reached his feet, still holding her, and faced Leigh. The little man had already brought up the rifle, was committed to firing the moment Wilde got up. The noise was deafening in the enclosed space, and the body Wilde was holding in front of him jerked, while in the same instant there came a crunch from the wall beside him. The bullet, fired at such close range from a high-velocity weapon, had passed right through Madeleine's chest to hit the ancient stone of the castle. Wilde could only gape at the woman in horror; she suggested a text-book example of the damage a bullet can do, as the expanding shot seemed to have blown away the entire front of her body. Blood soaked his legs, and her eyes were already dead as she slipped through his hands to the floor.

Leigh also stared at her in horror. "Oh, Christ," he said. "Oh, Christ."

The woman lay on the ground. Wilde stepped over her, reaching for Leigh. The rifle came back up, but too slowly. It could do nothing but wave from side to side in an attempt to keep off the enormous force looming at it. It struck Wilde across the side of the head and he did not even feel it. But Leigh was gone. He released the rifle butt and leapt on to the spiral stone stairs leading upwards. And disappeared.

Wilde stopped, to wipe sweat from his face, and some blood where the rifle had struck him. He felt dazed, the beating he had just taken combining with the exhaustion of the past twenty-four hours to make his head swing. Blood also dripped from his right forearm, but there was so much blood around it was impossible to decide which was his and which was Madeleine's.

He climbed slowly. The staircase clung to the wall, so he mounted several steps before he came in sight of the next floor. He could hear nothing above his own breathing and the scuffing of his feet on the old stone. But when he could see into the next level he paused to listen.

And still heard only his own breathing. He looked at another empty space, littered with dust and rat droppings, off which opened a rotting wooden door, sagging on its hinges.

He climbed again, reached the level, stood still, and then moved towards the door. He put his foot against it and pushed, and it fell right off the hinge and collapsed in a cloud of dust. He waited, and looked into what might once have been a bedchamber. It was gloomy, the only windows two arrow slits. Wilde stepped inside, muscles tensed, waiting for fingers to claw at his throat. But the room was empty.

He went outside, approached the next flight of steps. Once again he climbed slowly. And slowly his breathing was settling down, leaving only the white hot anger, the killing anger. And now he heard a sound. From above him there came a scraping. He threw himself to one side, reaching up to lodge his fingers on the floor above, hurling his body from the steps to swing over the stair well, leaving the passage clear. And just in time. A large stone came tumbling downwards, no doubt fallen from the roof in years gone by, and now propelled by Leigh to scatter across the steps, bounce on the floor beneath, and then crash through the well to the ground. And now feet stamped on his fingers, and he grunted with pain. But his legs were already swinging back to find the stairs, after that long dizzy moment when he had hung in space.

He looked up, and they stared at each other. Then Leigh turned again and ran for the last flight, leading to the roof. Wilde did not hurry. This was definitely the end of the line. He climbed slowly and methodically, placing one foot in front of the other, crossing the floor of the top-story chamber, and mounting towards the rectangle of blue sky which lay above.

Half-way up he checked, and listened. It was time for another missile, if Leigh could find one. But apparently there were no others. He heard no sound.

He reached the roof, stood in the warm sunlight and inhaled, gazed at Leigh. The little man crouched in one of the embrasures. "God damn you, Wilde," he said. "You should have been left, to rot yourself in Ibiza."

"It was all I had in mind," Wilde said.

"God damn you," Leigh said again, and pushed himself backwards.

Wilde did not go to the edge. Sixty feet was a long way, and there was only tumbled stone at the bottom of it. He sat down, and leaned his head on the wall, and gazed at the sun. The anger and the hate, the impulse to vicious violence had all left him as if someone had turned off a tap. He was only aware of his total exhaustion, of the number of bruises and cuts and sharp pains which covered his body, of the certainty that he could no more move a muscle than he could run a mile.

He closed his eyes.

V

A wooden ship has a smell all of its own. However overlaid by paint or varnish, or the aroma of diesel oil, it should yet be there, and it should be pleasant; if it is at all musty there is cause for concern.

This smell was pleasant. So was the motion, a gentle roll from side to side, and so was the noise, a steady throb from the engine room.

So was the company. Halma sat at the foot of his bunk, gazing at him. She did not appear to blink, until she was sure his eyes were open, then she both blinked and smiled.

Perhaps it had all been a dream. Except that he could not remember falling asleep. But the last time he had seen Halma had been when they had been buried alive together. Correction; he had not seen her then, either. But he could remember what she felt like.

And she was wearing her swim-suit, under a mutton-cloth blouse. Then where was the Prince?

"You are awake," she said, as if confirming this important fact to herself. "The Master will be pleased."

She was close enough to touch. He held her wrist. "Where am I?"

"On board the *Dingo,* Mr. Wilde."

"The *Dingo.*" Wilde thought about that. "Doing what?"

"You are lying down. And you must continue to lie down. You have not been well."

"I meant, where is the *Dingo* going, and what is she doing?"

"We are on our way round to Ajaccio," she explained. "It is the idea of the French police. They feel that they must make sure the Master becomes involved in no more mishaps until he is safely back in Xanda."

"How did you get out of the cave?"

"The French police opened the entrance, Mr. Wilde. They are very efficient."

"And how did I get here?"

"We found you in the tower, Mr. Wilde. That is, the French police found you. They are . . ."

"Very efficient. But exactly when was this?"

"This morning, Mr. Wilde."

"And it is now . . ."

"It will be dark in an hour. Mr. Smith Horton says that we should be in Ajaccio by then."

"And I have been out all of that time?"

"Well, Mr. Wilde, the police surgeon examined you, and diagnosed that you were suffering from total exhaustion, which could only be relieved by complete rest. So he gave you a sedative to make sure that you did not stir for some time. He was . . ."

"Very efficient. But there is a breakdown in this efficiency somewhere, Halma. Shouldn't I be in gaol? Or didn't the French police manage to discover the odd corpse up there?"

"Oh yes, Mr. Wilde. They were very upset."

"There's a likely story."

"They were very upset about the whole situation, Mr. Wilde," Halma said. "But when the Master explained who he was, they were even more upset. The thought of what had nearly happened to him, on French soil, was very upsetting."

"And they were so upset they didn't bother to take me into custody?"

"You have diplomatic immunity, Mr. Wilde. As a Xandan representative."

"As a . . ."

"I took the liberty of so describing you, Mr. Wilde," Walid said from the opposite bunk. Wilde turned so violently it was quite painful. "Oh, I have been here all the while," the Prince said. "I am not supposed to move about."

"And how is the leg?"

"Apparently it will heal, thanks to you. But I have lost a lot of blood, and it is probable I shall always walk with a limp. But believe me, I understand that you saved my life. You have but to ask of me, and it shall be yours."

"I wouldn't mind a drink," Wilde said.

"I will get it," Halma said, and left the cabin.

"You have made a considerable impression upon that girl," the Prince said. "I really do not see how she can any longer be of use to me."

"Now that is something I'd like to discuss," Wilde said. "You must understand, Excellency, that she was under considerable emotional stress in that cave. What is more, she genuinely supposed that she was about to die. People do strange things when they suppose they are about to die. You don't want to take any notice of her at all."

"On the other hand," the Prince said, apparently not having listened, "I seem to have at hand a ready replacement in Jonquil Malone. I take it you would have no objection to that, Mr. Wilde?"

Wilde goggled at him. "*You* propose to employ Jonquil Malone as a bodyguard?"

"Oh, she will have other duties as well. But she seems to think that she would be able to take care of my necessities. At least for a while."

Wilde sighed.

"Ah," the Prince said. "You do have some objections."

"I have no objections at all," Wilde said. "But I would like to have a word with her, if I may."

The Prince rang a little bell, and Jonquil came in with a glass. "I'm told to give you this," she said, and handed Wilde the freezing rum punch. "If that doesn't put strength back into your veins I don't know what will."

He sipped, and regarded her. She still wore her black bikini. "Sit down."

She hesitated, and then sat at the end of the Prince's bunk, exchanging a hasty smile with her new employer. "You don't want to get yourself excited, Jonas," she said. "You are really very done up. I suppose you are growing old, at that. When I remember . . ."

"That's my trouble," Wilde said. "Remembering."

"Ah," she said. "Yes. I suppose I owe you an explanation."

"It's an idea," Wilde said. "Otherwise . . ."

"Oh, you do carry on. I'm in the Prince's employ now. You can't lay a finger on me without upsetting the Master. I never realised before what a marvellous immunity that gives me."

"And just whose employ were you in before?"

"Ah," she said. "I was going to explain that, really. You may remember that once upon a time the Israelis and the British were pretty close."

"Once."

"Well, during that period I managed to form some good contacts inside the B.S.S. Did you know that Gerald Light and I once spent a weekend together?"

The boat was starting to roll. Or was that picture just beyond the scope of his imagination. "You're not going to stop now?"

"Well, everything I told you, when we first got together last week, was absolutely true. I just left out that I had been unhappy with the set-up, as controlled by Carmel, from the beginning. There was something not quite right about it, and I didn't like the way I wasn't allowed any contact with any other branch of the service. Only with my immediate superior. I put in for a transfer, and at the same time aired one or two opinions. Do you know, it just never got to anybody? I was told it had been turned down, of course, but the fact was that it had been siphoned off by Carmel, and when I tried to side-step her again it was once more intercepted, and I received a rap over the knuckles. So there I was, stuck in the middle of an assignment, entirely under the control of that blond zombie, unable to query any order. And not knowing what she was at. I became desperate. I mean, I knew she was up to something."

"So you contacted *my* boss?"

"Well, it seemed the only thing left to do. He was a little stiff at first, of course. Inclined to give me the brush-off. But when I explained the situation, and how I was sure it was linked with the Xandan problem, he suddenly became very interested indeed. He even remembered that you and I had worked together once, in the old days."

"By accident."

"On your part. I had been told to pick you up at Heathrow. So he suggested I pick you up again, and infiltrate you into the middle of them and see what happened. Putting Wilde in the middle of that lot, he said, will be rather like putting a fox into a hen-coop. Something will come flying out, and it may be useful."

"Good God," Wilde said. "You mean they knew where I was, all the time?"

"Of course they did, Jonas. You don't suppose Sir Gerald ever really lets you out of his sight, do you?"

"But when I started to contact London, when the Smith Hortons showed up . . ."

"I couldn't let on what I was at, Jonas. That was the one thing I had promised Sir Gerald would not happen." She smiled at him. "But Martha and I had a little chat while you and Mervyn were down in the oil. It was my idea they stick close. I told them to cruise the west coast of Corsica until they heard from us."

"What made you choose Corsica? The Prince could have gone in any direction."

"Save that I had an idea he would go where it was suggested he should go, and Corsica had cropped up in Carmel's briefings, more than once. It was the only lead I had, anyway. So I hunched on it."

"And nearly got us all killed."

"I assumed you could take care of things. Although you wouldn't have, would you, Jonas, if they hadn't locked me up with you. I think you should be very grateful."

"You had no idea I was just the first wave of the assault? That Bruno della Guardia was really Clement Leigh? That Madeleine was his prize agent?"

"Well, I do now. Carmel has been talking. This really was their final effort. They had lost too many people. So, they hoped you would be enough, but in any event, they figured you would generally unsettle all the Prince's security arrangements and have him feeling he had foiled another attempt on his life. Carmel and Bunty, and Steve, were really there to bail Clem and Madeleine out, if the going got rough. And they tried."

"And failed, thanks to Mr. Wilde," the Prince said. "The only thing Carmel has apparently not told us is precisely which country her group was working for, but I am sure we will be able to persuade her, in due course, to be more co-operative."

Wilde turned his head to look at him. But he addressed Jonquil. "And you are going to assist, in this persuasion, and all the other persuasions which will probably become necessary? What about Bunty?"

"Well," Jonquil said, a trifle sulkily. "They are both guilty of some pretty nauseating crimes themselves. Anyway . . ." She smiled at the Prince. "I would hope to be able to persuade the Master to temper his justice with mercy."

"I wish you luck," Wilde said. "Do you think I could have another drink?"

She took the glass and stood up. "I think you're just jealous. I'm going to be head of the Xandan Secret Service. I'll be an equal of Sir Gerald. Whereas you . . ."

"Are just an employee," Wilde agreed. "It's slightly better for the conscience. Just tell me one last thing, Jonquil. Having found me and got me working again, had you by any chance promised to deliver me back to the fold?"

"Oh, I don't know anything about that," she said, her eyes wide and innocent behind the horn-rimmed spectacles. "You'll have to talk to Mervyn Smith Horton. I'll get your drink."

She closed the door behind her. The Prince was still smiling. "Do you know, Mr. Wilde, I think you are really very fond of that young woman. This encourages me. I am sure that I also will become very fond of her. And I am sure that she will be good for me. She may even have a . . . how shall I put it? A civilising influence upon my administration? But I am also sure that there is no need for you two to part. Listen. I have chartered an aircraft which is standing by at Ajaccio, and which will fly me and my crew and my, ah, employees, back to Xanda. We will be there by tomorrow morning. I'd be very grateful if you would accompany us."

Wilde sighed, and closed his eyes. "Would I be senior to Miss Malone?"

"You, Mr. Wilde, I would make head of my entire armed forces, of which the Secret Service is only a part."

"I shall treasure the thought, Excellency. But I'm afraid I can't accept. I don't think the Queen would ever agree."

"My dear fellow, I will speak with her the next time I am in London."

"I wouldn't," Wilde said. "About me, I mean. Just let's say that, in case of need, no doubt Jonquil will know where to find me."

The Prince gazed at him for some seconds. "Ah, well, Mr. Wilde. I was told this would be your decision. Yet I cannot let you slip away into obscurity without some tangible evidence of my great, my undying gratitude for all you have done for me, and for my country. I am going to present you with one of my most valuable possessions."

"Now wait a moment," Wilde said. "I travel very light, and often in great discomfort. Extra baggage just isn't on."

"She will care for you and fight for you and die for you, if need be, Mr. Wilde," Walid said. "And she will look after you, at all things. I will not take no for an answer." He watched the door opening. "In any event, she can no longer work for me, in view of everything that has happened, and I cannot just turn her out into the world. She has no knowledge of the world, beyond Xanda. You will have to teach her."

Halma carried a fresh glass of rum punch. "I have brought your drink, Master."

"*I*," Wilde said sadly, "have to teach *you?*"